NEOTENICA

NEOTENICA
JOON OLUCHI LEE

Nightboat Books
New York

ISBN: 978-1-64362-020-6

Cover art by Catherine Homans
Design and typesetting by Brian Hochberger
Text set in Desire and Janson

Cataloging-in-publication data is available
from the Library of Congress

Nightboat Books
New York
www.nightboat.org

Table of Contents

RO-S/S-14

Young Ae's husband, who still had several months to become Young Ae's husband, had huge feet and a little, dainty penis. A few years before, while living in New York, never once had he had to watch the proverbial gap between the train and the platform because his big long feet never had a chance of slipping through and getting caught in that gap which was neither too wide nor too narrow. His little penis did not, as the condition seemed to dictate to some gay men, force him into a life of sexual bottoming. He was a top, myopically and obliviously so. Of course, it helped that while he did enjoy, once in a while, relatively anonymous sex with gay men, he was heterosexual. Young Ae's future husband loved sticking his dainty, rather pretty erection up soft tight buttholes. Young Ae's vagina was elegant and near Medieval in its snugness, but it was nothing like the hard bubble of a sphincter. What's more, he guessed correctly that Young Ae would not really like him to fuck her in the anus. Doggy style, yes (he sometimes felt she did not like looking at his face), but never up the butt. And he loved fucking buttholes; to him, it was like fucking a dimple. And he never felt embarrassed about the smallness of his penis when he demanded his sex partner to bend over, even when some bitchy bottoms giggled at his dick. He ignored it and pierced away anyway. His cock was little but got very hard when hard, and the bottom was usually surprised and pleasured. Young Ae's future husband was preternaturally something of a rebel, and hanging on him, the resulting smugness could be, to some, a bit adorable.

The BART train was empty but for him, so he sprawled his body out on one of the seats facing the door reserved for the handicapped and elderly. Usually he was very conscientious about special needs seats, but not tonight. He was on his way home to San Francisco from a house party in Oakland that Young Ae felt was beneath her.

"If I wanted to get squeezed between a bunch of dudes and get my clothes soaked with pot and body odor, I would just build a time machine and go back to college," Young Ae had said without feeling as he dressed for the party. Her left fingers were squeezing a cigarette, and she was ashing so rapidly that teeny embers were burning teeny holes into the angora-and-cashmere Rick Owens cardigan she was wearing. She was standing in the doorway of his bathroom, striking a pose meant to be both seductive and blockading, even though her body was too reedy for blockading. As for seductive: Young Ae's future husband was growing sexually tired of her, as beautiful as she was. As he slumped in the train, he hoped that she would be gone by the time he got home; he preferred to finish off his high by yanking on his hard little penis with his own hand. But no matter: the party had been fun: he reeked of marijuana, beer and dudes.

As the train pulled into West Oakland, Young Ae's future husband realized that he hadn't been reading the open book on his lap at all, but rather staring deep into the framed advertisement for a new online dating service called "Nerve." He bent his head again into the book but the printed words just looked like the color red to him. His eyes were very dark, his skin powder-pale. He had very coarse hair that he blow-dried every day, even though the '80s were long over, as Young Ae reminded him. He had a smallish head that looked too small for the rest of his body, which was quite big-boned. He was tall and narrow, with a muscular chest and just a touch of a gut. He also had big arms that looked out of proportion with the rest of his body. But he definitely had the face of a thin, narrow person, with big shelves of cheekbones that made his face look wasted, even as a child. But his chin was flat, his jawline square and ugly. He was 28 years old, and Korean American.

Sometimes you think that the way you look will protect you from the dangers of the world. You think, for instance, that since you are a relatively tall male person, wearing a big white t-shirt and baggy khaki shorts and brick-heavy Jordans, that you have a tough inside that comes through for the outside world as not just tough, but more than tough: Street. This is what Young Ae's future husband thought. But if you could have punctured his soul with a small hollow needle you would have found that the stuff inside was as soft as buttercream but without cake sweetness. He thought he was radiating Street sitting there, sprawled out not in attitude or entitlement but rather beer fuzz and pot buzz, as the train pulled into West Oakland and the group of young black men came on, and proceeded to beat him up.

But when Young Ae's future husband first saw the teenagers come in through the doors of the train car, he didn't think of any racist words like "gang." He thought: Army. There were five or six of them but they felt like nine or ten. He could pick them apart by their heads and movements, but they seemed to be moving in unison, towards a point. They were dressed in a way that made you think they were wearing exactly the same thing, but in fact they were just wearing three unremarkable colors: beige, grey and white. One of them wore a soft do-rag. At least one had long hair that was neither braided nor dreaded, so that it wafted around him, licorice candy floss. The clothes had a looseness that denoted comfort more than racist stereotype. Each guy wore one color from head to toe, so you couldn't tell where shirt stopped and pants began. You couldn't even really see hands, let alone fists. Their faces were angry but not in a way that you felt threatened; they just seemed as if they were collectively in a bad mood, and particularly the kind you couldn't blame them for. Most days, Young Ae's husband himself felt as if he were in an ongoing bad mood for which no one could blame him, so seeing this army didn't alarm him in any way.

The army was so soft the punches shouldn't have hurt at all, but they did. Fists landed hard but the skin of each was calm and silken, flawless as that of mythical youth. Without bone and kinetic energy, they would have surely been caresses. Their faces didn't move, they didn't make a sound. They just began punching the future husband of Young Ae. Because he was already sprawled out, the punches quite literally flattened him. He lay across two seats as the punches came leisurely, all together, all at once and without speed in a way that rocked him to sleep and pain. The young men stomped their feet with their heavy shoes on the weak carpeted floor while they beat him, and although Young Ae's future husband was tall and strong enough to not just block but hit back, he chose not to. He let those big arms lay still, connected to his narrow shoulders and long torso. He was big-armed and low-titted: he had rosy, big, perpetually hard cone-shaped nipples, and their sharp tips were pointed downward and attached low on over-exercised pecs so that it looked a little as though he had breasts. He made a half-hearted attempt to protect his head with his book but that was so silly; one of the army giggled, grabbed the book and flung it over his shoulder, but there were no bridesmaids behind him.

The trip between West Oakland and Embarcadero stations takes less than ten minutes. The army of young men in grey, beige, and white beat Young Ae's future husband for a good four minutes in the pitch black of the tunnel that goes under the Bay, and Young Ae's future husband almost fell asleep underneath the Bay and the punches. He decided to give in totally, and lay down fully, spine relaxed, arms out, one knuckle dragging the floor, both hands open in a Jesus Christ pose, coccyx dovetailing comfortably into the curve of the tough fabric seat. He didn't know what made the army want to pounce on him but he knew the feelings that came out of them. It had something to do with West Oakland. It wasn't anything about bullets, though; it wasn't anything about guns or old cars wearing chrome stilettos. It wasn't about welfare, it wasn't about no fathers, it wasn't about Rodney King. It wasn't about cops, it wasn't about bags of pot or fat bottles of malt liquor with dumb obscene names. It wasn't about Hunter's Point, it wasn't about the predator and the prey. It wasn't about low-income housing, it wasn't about GEDs. It wasn't about AIDS, it wasn't about babymamas. It wasn't about the war in Iraq and it wasn't about the overcrowded prison system that seemed to encircle the entire peaceful, still hippy-dippy Bay Area. It wasn't about history and it wasn't about hate.

The train pulled into Embarcadero and no one was waiting to get in. The doors slid open without any emotion and the army had already moved into another car lightly, as a pack of angels. Loudly, they ran in grace. Off they ran, in grace, leaving Young Ae's future husband like a homeless drunk or a drunk yuppie at the end of a long, boring night. It wasn't until Civic Center station that someone came in, saw that he wasn't homeless or a yuppie, just a drunk dude who'd been beaten up. They helped him up and out of the train.

As Young Ae's future husband sat on the steps leading up to Civic Center Plaza, two BART Police officers came and took his statement which was: I didn't see who beat me up. The cops looked at him with total incredulity, but while the white one looked just plain fatigued, the Chinese one got mad at him.

"How could you have not seen who beat you up?"

"I was asleep. I had my eyes closed. I was a little drunk, I was at a party, which is why I took the BART home."

"You were asleep while someone punched your face."

"Yeah. I just told you."

"We don't believe you. What are you trying to hide?"

"I'm not trying to hide anything."

"We don't believe you. And you may not care who did this to you, but you should care that they might do this to someone else, your daughter or your sister or your mother or your girlfriend, and you can prevent it."

"I don't believe in crime prevention. And I don't have a sister or daughter or girlfriend. So unless you want to arrest me for getting beat up I'd like you to leave me alone."

The two cops shook their heads, smirking and shrugging with one other. They both had fat thick necks but if Young Ae's future husband had stood up, he would have stood a full head taller than both of them. They muttered some stuff that Young Ae's future husband couldn't make out because his right ear was swollen and filled with blood. But when they were nearing the other end of the long station, one of them turned around and said, quietly and audibly: "Faggots."

Young Ae's future husband stood up and said to the little, primly-dressed black woman who was hurrying into the MUNI gate, "Did you hear that?" The woman ignored him. Finding himself alone in the station, he took out his own MUNI pass. Originally, he had planned to take the BART all the way to 24th Street and walk, but it would be simpler at this point to take the J train. When he sat near the woman to wait for the J, she got up and walked further down the platform. Young Ae's future husband sat with his head between his knees. Now, it all hurt so much. His bones were not broken but they felt shattered, not like bones but chocolate: the instant they went to bits, the bits melted into a goo that became sugar and dirt. Then he realized that he didn't have his book with him. It was Young Ae's copy of *Beloved*. She had four other copies besides, but he knew she would still be upset.

He looked down at his upside down stomach and saw the t-shirt he had ironically put on for the party. He bought it years ago at the Anarchist Bookstore: a white hand-silk screened bootleg number bearing an image of Madonna peeling herself out of a black leather jacket, atop of a big fat acid-pink triangle. Underneath, a quote set soberly in Times New Roman: "Every straight guy should have a man's tongue in his mouth at least once." Young Ae's future husband laughed, and ingots of blood landed on Madonna's bustier and the word "at." He suddenly remembered that one member of the army actually had a slash of pink across his beige t-shirt that made him look like a rare vegetable, split open as for a snack. Until the train came, right on time this time, he quietly and gently fucked that pink memory.

A BOOK ABOUT BELOVED

Young Ae was a PhD. student in English, and she studied and worked hard at her research (metaphors of dance and choreography in Toni Morrison's novels) so that her innards might be worthy of their shell she worked so hard to make beautiful, supple, strong yet soft. But in her bedroom, inside her armoire close to the front was a black rainproof duffle bag containing beat-up toe shoes, leotards frayed at the crotch and armpit sweat stains like tie-dye, and one beautiful costume, white as cake, in a Chloé garment bag. The costume was from her time with the *corps* of *Giselle*. Inside its bodice was a cloth label that said: "San Francisco Ballet Company. Giselle. Role: Willi 16. Miss Thomas. Miss Kang. Ms. Whitford. Ms. Williams. Ms. Lee. Ms. Tanemura." The names had been written in by hand, with black or blue ink, variations in penmanship and ink color dependent upon the costumer.

Young Ae had stolen the costume on her last day with the company, zipping it fast into the garment bag containing a new expensive dress she had just picked up from Saks. She felt guilty and a little mean, but as she had always been a tad kleptomaniac, didn't act upon the moral feeling. The expensive dress now hung in the closet carelessly, while its garment bag still wrapped itself around the Willi costume with possessiveness in the oily duffle bag, the whole thing together content and lightweight like the corpse of a well-loved pet.

Somewhere within a variable radius of the armoire was her husband, who was unemployed. Or as he liked to put it, "Unemployed At the Moment." She wished he were as indispensable to society as he thought of himself. In the JPEG through which she first saw him, he looked handsome enough. In 147 KB his square jaw didn't look as blocky it did in real life. She supposed that most people might find a square jaw sexy on a man; she herself did not. Young Ae had figured that 500 x 694 was a reliable enough resolution. In that pic, she had liked how his mischievous, boyish grin went together with the humorlessness in his eyes.

Young Ae had decided to enter into an arranged marriage because: she had grown tired of dating men who disappointed her in escalating quantity and quality, she was not a lesbian, and she was deathly afraid at the thought of living alone. She thought a digitalized arranged marriage was as legitimately random as an internet dating site. On their first date, Young Ae's future husband took her to see a revival house screening of *Scarface*. She had dressed carefully carelessly, in a plain knee-length black box-pleated skirt she bought at a thrift store and an old black wool sweater from J. Crew. It was a man's crewneck sweater, and the only thing revealing about it was a small hole near the hip; it could have been a moth hole or a snag hole. From a certain advantage, the hole showed a bit of the slip she wore underneath. Young Ae's future husband noticed the hole right away, stuck his finger in it and fingered it, stretching it deftly.

"You've got a hole here," he said soberly.

"I know," she matched his sober tone, although she could have easily gone flirty and giggly.

"I like this shirt you're wearing under it. It's very pale orange. With little raised dots."

Young Ae didn't say thank you, even though she liked how he exactly identified the shade and pattern of the slip. She replied, "It *is* a very pale orange. And the dots *are* raised." When she first spotted him standing by the box office of the movie theatre, she had wanted to burst out laughing because he was wearing the same J. Crew sweater. They didn't talk about that fact that night or thereafter, but she never forgot it.

"Do you like this movie?" he asked, assuming she'd already seen it.

"No. But then, I've never seen it. I don't like violence."

He shrugged and gave her her ticket. "In films or in real life?"

"I don't know." This was true; suddenly, she didn't know. It was a good second question for a first date. She noticed that he had a vague stink, gross but not repellant, rather like a puppy's mouth.

He told her what she already knew, that he was a first-year law student at Boalt Hall. He wanted to do social policy work, even though his mother, being an immigrant from Korea, wanted him to go high corporate. His acquiescence to the matchmaking was a way of throwing her off the trail while he spent the summer doing unpaid work in a public defender's office up in Sonoma County rather than a paid internship at one of the big downtown firms.

"And you're a ballet dancer?" he asked.

"Yes. Or I was."

"Your profile says you are."

"San Francisco isn't exactly the peak of the ballet world. And I broke my second toe too many times. It's longer than my big toe. So this is the first official year of my retirement."

"So you're retiring because of your injury, not because of San Francisco."

It was not a question, but she treated it as one and replied yes. She hoped she didn't sound bitter or stupid but thought she probably sounded both bitter and stupid. He didn't seem to mind either way. They watched the film in silence; she hated it. As she anticipated, it was full of violence, not just loud guns that were even louder because of the remastering, but the ugly swaggering of men. However, she was struck by Michelle Pfeiffer, whose beauty was of a morbid kind. In slippery dresses, you could see her sternum and its thin surrounding bones radiating, but they did not indicate the ascetic musculature that Young Ae was used to with her ballet comrades. Young Ae wondered if her own muscular but skeletal body would melt down into a body like Pfeiffer's once she really settled into her retirement. She wondered if she would dance still—take classes, install a barre at home, join a modern dance troupe? She doubted it because she was not one of these dancers who chanted proudly, morbidly: "I'd rather die than stop dancing." Young Ae remembered a fairly famous principle dancer in her company who was forced into retirement a few years back. It was not an early retirement because the dancer was 42, so obviously she had hung on using every bit of talent, stubbornness and denial available to her, but in the end, her hip was messed up beyond repair. At the farewell party after her final performance, the dancer cried so, and kept chanting, "I'd rather die than stop dancing." Young Ae had wondered then if she would actually die, and in her head, mildly dared the dancer to suicide. But the dancer did not kill herself; instead, she transformed herself into a modern dancer. Young Ae went to see her perform in this new incarnation, and the dancer was good, but she still moved like an old ballet dancer rather than a modern dancer; there was a beautiful stiffness in her motion that Young Ae felt would never leave her. Still, the dancer was ecstatic at the party after that performance. Her new incantation was: "I knew I'd die if I couldn't dance. This is so great because it lets me focus on what I can do rather than what I can't."

She thought all this but had no chance to verbalize it as her future husband did not ask for her thoughts on the film once the house lights came up. Instead, they walked to dinner at an expensive vegetarian restaurant and made even smaller talk. But she didn't care. He paid the bill using his silence and swiftness as a battering ram through her minor but authentic protests. Outside, they had already agreed to go on a second date when she impulsively asked him if he wanted to come back to her apartment for a drink, and he accepted. He guessed accurately that she wanted to fuck him, and when they got near her bed to undress he was gratified by her brusqueness, her nonchalant lack of coquettishness.

Young Ae stood naked and watching while her future husband undressed. She enjoyed the sight of his body; naked, he looked like what he looked like dressed. He looked strong but with relaxed edges. She could tell that his shoulders were narrow, but the deltoids were big and muscular, creating a nicer illusion. His arms and legs were long and muscular without being too cut. His chest wasn't as built as his arms although they too looked muscular, curved at the edges with dark taut nipples that pierced her when he fucked her on top of her. Where the pectoral muscle met the armpit you could see strength and toughness, two ribs arching into the middle of his abdomen. But his belly was soft, an innie belly button made deeper by the slightest of a beer belly that extended into the beginning of love handles at his waist. (Teacup handles, Young Ae thought.) He should have been pear-shaped, yet he wasn't. From where she looked at him, he looked flat, squat and long at the same time. His body was the kind that should be packed into a shiny, brightly colored, ironically sophomoric spandex singlet and sat behind a drum kit in a rock band otherwise made entirely of females.

She was turning away from him to get the condoms she kept in her drawer when he asked: "Do you have condoms? Sorry I didn't bring any with me."

"Yes, I have some."

"Good. I mean, I know I don't need them but you don't know that. I don't have any STDs."

"Well, having no STDs doesn't mean you are infertile."

"That's true. Sorry. I guess I'm pretty confident about pulling out. But you're right."

"You should probably still pull out but let's use a condom anyway."

"OK. I really want to fuck you right now," he said.

"Yes. I want to fuck you too," she said.

Before they agreed to marry, Young Ae felt she had to tell him the truth about her ballet career. It felt important to her, but it was also small on the grand scale of revelations. By that time he had revealed to her that once or twice a month, he liked to scan Craigslist for gay men who would suck his cock. The way he said the words to her made it clear that it was *not* a confession, although his tone was not dispassionate. Since by this time they had confirmed that he actually had no STDs and was HIV negative, Young Ae blandly asked if he were gay, or bisexual.

"I don't think so. I don't fantasize about men or dicks or anything. I simply get off on the dirtiness of the act," he answered. He did not offer to cease this behavior, nor did she ask. It seemed reasonable enough to her; having been around enough straight male dancers who acted gayer than her gay male friends, Young Ae was neither mortified nor dejected, although she was not quite sure why she was so nonplussed, either. She couldn't tell if she felt accepting or indifferent. They had been going for meals and walks together, having sex and watching movies for more than a few months. They knew they were trawling along towards marriage.

She chose a Sunday evening and waited for him in his apartment. He had given her a copy of his keys not because he loved her, but because he was just the kind of guy to be loose and fancy-free with his keys. As far as Young Ae knew, sets of his apartment keys were held by a couple law school friends (one of whom was also his pot dealer), a buddy from college, one of his three younger brothers and his mother. Stacks of donuts and snacks, and Tupperwares of home-cooked Korean food magically appeared and disappeared, often without his ever touching or noticing them. His apartment was a spacious luxury loft that looked as if it couldn't bear to have anything to do with luxury. It had been lulled into submission by his radical indifference to material objects. Things had no meaning for him, monetary or emotional. He had no television, no videos or video player, no video game consoles, no framed photographs of people, no art on the walls, not even cheesy prints or posters, and except his law textbooks, no books. This last thing truly shocked her. She had been out with guys who had very few or very stupid books, but never no books. Rather than turning her off, however, this fascinated her. He did have a black MacBook that sat on his lap quite frequently and two shelves of records, mostly old obscure hip-hop singles, but if he had a turntable, she'd never seen it. He had only two pieces of furniture in the apartment: a long, low coffee table made of aluminum and a convertible sofa from the 1970s. He slept on the convertible and every morning, tucked it back in. He was fastidious about not leaving it open when he wasn't using it as a bed.

Young Ae was sitting on it when he finally came in. He switched the light on, saw her, and expressed no surprise.

"Hey, what's up."

"Hey. I wanted to talk to you but couldn't reach you so I thought I'd just come over."

"Cool." He plopped down next to her and looked straight into her eyes. It could have been alarming, but it wasn't.

"I thought you should know that I'm not really retiring from ballet because of my injuries. I mean, the injuries are real, but I could still dance. I'm quitting because I know that I'm not naturally strong or rhythmic enough to ever rise from the *corps*. I love dancing but not enough to endure it as a badge of my mediocrity."

She wanted to add that working with her body sometimes made her feel like a hooker, but chewed her lip instead. She didn't intend to be cute, but the gesture made her look cute.

"OK," he replied.

"I know it seems a small thing but I wanted to tell you because I didn't want you to think that I wanted you to think I was trying to impress you or your family by pretending to be some prima ballerina. I'm not."

"A prima ballerina? Or pretending?"

"Both."

"OK. It really doesn't matter to me, but I'm glad you don't feel the need to pretend. I really hate that."

Young Ae told him that she wanted to go back to school and figure out something else to do. She guessed that he guessed she wanted to marry a reasonable-looking man with a comfortable income to support her artistic and intellectual adventures. Her guess was right, because he was a man who wanted to devote his life to himself without becoming the freak antisocial uncle around his brothers' already procreative families. Nagging is a Korean national pastime and cultural heritage, and he wanted the freedom to be as freaky as he liked, with a pretty person by his side.

She understood. He liked marijuana and the occasional anonymous blowjob from gay men, but these vices seemed to balance his fanatical but sincere devotion to social justice. They didn't have much to talk about but they had good sex, found each other inoffensive, and liked each other's course in life. He fully supported her goal of graduate school. "You'll never work as a waitress," he told her. And she didn't. In addition to a respectably sized Cartier diamond of her choice, he bought her four Balenciaga Lariat bags: two in the basic tissue-thin, crackling lambskin (one black, the other an army green), another in black suede, and the last in milky canvas printed with blue pastoral scenes, like a tea service. They had no honeymoon but she was happier with beautiful things anyway.

BUDDHISM FOR MATERIALISTS

There is a young boy longing for a puppy; it is not an unusual image. There, too, is a woman scolding her young son; that, too, is not an unusual image. Now put the two together: the young boy longs for a puppy and his mother scolds him for it. She is young for a woman with four children: she's not even 35, her eldest is not quite 10. That might be the reason her face has collapsed a decade early, since she doesn't abuse any alcohol or drugs, never touched a cigarette to her lips, not even for a girlish jaunt of a puff, and she will die without having smoked a single cigarette. The early collapse of her face makes her seem imperious and impervious. As a girl, she had large moony eyes that made her whole face shimmer, made her average nose and mouth seem avid and trembling. But her parents are no longer alive and her husband has just left her for another woman, so there is no one around her to remember that girl. Instead, when her eldest boy looks into her face, he only sees the collapse: everything soft in her face, the eyeballs, the lips, the important pockets of cute fat in the cheeks, even the lime-flavored Jell-O cartilage of her nose, all shriveled and shrunk, receded away from the world into the recesses of her interior. The final effect was to make her face seem all bone, with barely any skin stretched over it. Some might have found it beautiful; others might have seen it as an ancient occult mask or a football helmet; no one would have said it was pretty. Her eldest son, looking up at her face, certainly does not find it beautiful, pretty, or a mask, but it intimidates him, as when he looked at images of the bone-white rubble of ancient temples and senatoriums that become monuments.

"You are being selfish. What kind of example are you setting for your brothers? You are the oldest and you are crying for no reason. Look at your brothers. Look at how strong they are even though they are younger and smaller than you. Look at the smallest. You should learn from him. I'm ashamed of you. Stop crying."

The mother scolds in a level speaking voice but to some people listening it sounds like screaming. She isn't addicted to any chemical substance but her own feeling of anger at the world. This woman's young son, the young boy longing for a puppy, will be Young Ae's husband. He lets go. He is standing in front of a mobile dog-adoption unit: a large white RV that has sides that slide up to reveal two levels of small cages containing cute adorable adoptable puppies and small dogs who have been rescued from abuse or abandonment. The young boy might see himself in not just the particular four-month Chihuahua-Hound-Rottweiler he clung to, but all the dogs, young and old, who are displayed from the scrolled-up passenger side of the shelter RV that afternoon, except already he has a hard little kernel of self-worth that repelled self-pity. But in his tears, he doesn't know it. His mother is right: he is crying with the fierceness of self-centered greed, the fury at the injustice of disappointment. He wants to hold that wet-eyed thing, his heart is drawn to it and he wants to take it home, he wants to own it, care for it, love it, be near it all its days. When he approaches the dog, it jumps at him, as if it were trying to claw through the white-washed wire cage whose grates are just wide enough for contact but not escape. Instinctively, the boy reaches out and grabs the pup's paw: it's hot, soft, vibrating, nervous and ferocious, all at once. Had he known the word "beautiful," he would use it.

The mother pulls her first-born away from the dog, gently. The few people gathered around the puppy-van notice nothing of note, and certainly nothing sinister. There might have been someone who feels uneasy for the young boy, but that person is at home today. The mother doesn't care what people think of her or her parenting, because she is confident in the superiority of her mothering. For instance, her pull of her boy is gentle, not at all a yank, but no one could know that she held hands with her oldest son only when she needed to yank him, gently. No one could know she squeezes his hand so hard that the glossy beige tips of her finely done French manicure cut into his palm like a switchblade. Of course later she cleans the wound vociferously, half-wondering, half-chiding, one hundred percent impatient: "What could you have been doing, what dangerous thing were you playing with, to get such a cut? What am I going to do with you?"

+

For the reading of her mother-in-law's will, Young Ae does not subvert or rebel but acts the role of the bourgeois Korean housewife. She puts on a high-necked dress made of dark double-faced wool, with sleeves to her wrists and skirt to her knees, and her hair twisted up into a classic chignon, held together not with thin threadlike hairpins that set off the airport security, but clamped with one faux-tortoise shell banana comb. Young Ae's husband also acts a, or rather the, part: a very appropriate suit for a heterosexual man: dark and just slightly ill-fitting. But underneath his crispy-white Brooks Brothers shirt, with its collar buttons fastened tight against the expensive thick silk necktie, he has on an old white t-shirt with the cracked graphic of Fritz the Cat's X-rated girlfriend, grinning her hash-haze meow between cheap blond hair and lux plush bosom. The shirt's armpits are stained by years of old sweat and the striations of yellow circlets emanate right to the front of the shirt. But the sweat stains are scalloped and shaded from dark golden piss-yellow to pale daffodil-yellow, so it looks like curious embroidery done in urine-shined metallic thread, or as special as any Bedazzler or Swarovski crystal beads.

+

The young boy who would be Young Ae's husband watches from behind as his mother and three brothers walk in upright intimacy. His mother is not the type to cuddle and coddle, especially in public, but as she moves forward with her boys, pushing with one hand the huge stroller containing her magnificently-behaved four-year-old, the other hand holding the hand of her five-year-old who in turn clings to the six-year-old, there is nevertheless something touching in the undulating synchronicity of their movement. Ten paces back, the eldest boy's hand throbs but in his mind is involuntary admiration at the strength of his mother and unified brothers. So he keeps watching the four people from the distance carefully and quietly maintained by the boy himself. She seems to like it this way and he is OK with that. He can't remember when he stopped being afraid of getting separated from his mother in public places, but now, that specific fearlessness is both a propeller and a destiny.

+

Young Ae feels it is a strange kind of play they are all acting in. Everyone in the room is improvising not in liberation but desperation, flailing towards a script, a text to which they could yield their bodies and make sense of it all. Eight people sit around an enormous round table waiting for the lawyer to come in and read the will. Young Ae keeps bumping her knee against the ugly knobby leg of the table. She looks around her and sees that everyone looks the same, regardless of gender or race or age, all blank, all covered in oddly-fitting blackness. She remembers when her mother-in-law was dying, the four brothers and their four spouses were summoned to the small but exclusive beach resort town her mother-in-law had chosen as her place of eventual death. Because she was rich enough, Young Ae's mother-in-law didn't need to go into a rest home. Rather, she rented a chic, modern beach house gleaming with walls of bulletproof glass, expensive tiling and filled with kitchen appliances as metallic and pointing as rockets. (She despised old buildings.) She hired a pricey hospice nurse named Kiernan who was white, female, under 30, chipper, pretty and freckled; she looked like one of the brothers' wives. But it was another, the wife of the youngest brother, a little thing with a little voice, who suggested that the wives gather one late morning to "catch up." This was funny since the four brothers rarely exchanged even holiday cards and never talked to one another on the phone, but also funnily appropriate for that precise reason. Young Ae is the wife of the eldest brother but also the newest wife. She can barely tell the other three women apart, including the white one. But she went, and so did the other wives because they knew what they would and needed to talk about: money and property.

Still waiting for the lawyer, still bumping her knee repeatedly against the table leg, Young Ae remembers her husband stomping back to their hotel room in the beach town, exhausted from an audience with his family. His voice cracked with rare extreme emotion:

"Is she even dying? As usual, she spent the whole night lecturing me about how I've fucked up my life and what a disappointment I am. How could I quit law school, blah blah. Then even you! Cold, frigid, infertility, blah blah. Unbelievable! I reminded her that we met through her Korean marriage bullshit website, a fact which she ignored. And my brothers all stood around beaming. Jesus."

That evening, Young Ae had felt guilty for her immediate thought, which was not being offended about falsely perceived as infertile, or perhaps correctly, as unemotional, but the same miserable thought she has right now, in her weirdly-fitting black dress, though now there is less guilt and more fatigue with her own preoccupations: when her husband's mother dies, her husband will probably get next to nothing—if not nothing at all.

+

The mother whips out a collapsible shopping cart from the back of the stroller. She unfolds it with the snap of a martial artist and loads it with lobsters and crabs. She has bought an entire tank from the fishmonger at the grocery store, and because this is a relatively downmarket market, the crustaceans are few and pretty feeble-looking. But weary as they are of living, they're still snapping. The woman's oldest son peers into the tank from a respectable distance as the creatures are scooped up with rubber gloved hands. The rubber is oxblood red and looks to the boy like a horror film pressed rewind: the spew of blood seems to reach forth and pull the animals into slasher death. A crab doesn't have the big wet eyes of a puppy, but the boy finds them huggable anyway. It's something about the way they move: not to get to any place different, but almost as if they are shaking their limbs out to remind themselves that they are living. The boy moves in closer and sees the small, slippery flesh that joins the hard violet-sheened shells. He can't imagine that these are the points at which humans aim pressure, knifepoint or teeth-point, to suck out the even more slippery and yielding flesh within, but he can intuit vulnerability. He imagines what it might be to hug this crab, with its micromovements, that feels even more miniature because it is fatigued, because it can't move very quickly, because when it snaps its claws there is no snap at all but just treading stale water.

When the mother and her four boys get to the more expensive market, they will get bigger and stronger crustaceans, ones that have more fight left in them, ones less philosophical and introspective about their reality as food. And she wants the ones with more will-to-life. At the bigger store, they find the livelier and more desperate shellfish. She also takes seven whole fish—four flounders and three very expensive sea bass. When the fishmonger asks if she wants them filleted, she replies, "No thank you. We are not going to eat them."

+

As they wait for the lawyer to arrive, Young Ae and her husband chat in small morse-code sentences, whispering as if they are in Study Hall.

"I think I will probably get nothing."

"Maybe."

"I think so. She's been threatening it for years."

"I know, but to cut you off completely...it seems so strange."

They are not looking at each other but straight on, so that while they whisper to one another they are sharing perspective, looking at the nose of the third brother, who is extremely handsome, and that of his wide-faced wife.

"I told you about the dog."

"Yes," Young Ae confirms; she knows the story.

"She thinks she's such a good person. Who tells their kid that they are allergic to dogs when they aren't? Just because she doesn't like dogs she has to put the blame on me?"

"Yes, crazy."

+

They visit four markets in total. As they emerge from the car, the mother has the cart with bags of wriggling crustaceans, and the oldest two boys are each carrying bags of dead unfilleted fish. The car is parked in a lot between an interstate highway that lulls as it goes through town and the beach. The parking lot extends several long blocks, almost the entire length of the beach. The mother's car sits at one end where the beach is rocky and thus usually more isolated. Pale grey sand has invaded much of the lot, making it beautiful. The thorns of speckled concrete have been worn down by the grains of sand, and gained a serene paleness that makes it look sisterly to sand, the way it was always meant to be.

It is December and the middle of the day in the middle of the week so there are only a couple other cars besides the mother's, and on the beach itself there is no one. Lugging the bought sea creatures, the mother leads her kids down to the edge of the water. There, she takes off her shoes. She pulls out the topmost bag in her cart and wades out a few feet into the water with silk-hosed feet. She turns the bag upside down in front of her. The brothers, supervised by the eldest, watch their mother. The eldest two see nothing new; they are used to this, the third is getting used to it, and the fourth will in another year or so. To the eldest boy, his mother looks as though she is dumping garbage; when she turns the bag upside down to let loose the crustaceans she holds her arm straight out in front of her at a perfect right angle to her upright body. To him, it looks like the body of someone forced to handle something gross, and he feels that if she were to hold her nose the picture would make sense. But he knows she isn't throwing out garbage. She is freeing the animals, liberating the creatures.

"These animals were all once human, and after we die, we too may become these animals. We have to respect their lives so they respect ours."

Even then, the boy thinks: It's weird to want to not harm something only because you don't want to become that thing capable of being harmed. He watches his mother complete her weekly ritual, plastic bag by plastic bag, coming back and forth from her spot in the ocean to her boys at the edge of the beach. When she has emptied the last plastic bag she stands and looks far off into the horizon. She gathers her hands in front of her, palm touching upright palm in prayer pose, and bows deeply, three and a half times, in three directions. Then she is done. Much, much later, the boy learns words like "reincarnation," "Nirvana" and "Karma." She's so devoted she even dumps the already dead fish into the sea.

+

The lawyer is an elegant older Korean man. He has just enough fat on him to glisten with prosperity, to keep him from looking haggard. He wears expensive titanium-framed glasses in a discreet oblong shape. His haircut is expensive: thick grey hair is swept dramatically off his forehead and sculpted into a pleasing curve. It looks like an updated version of a haircut he might have had as a rude and rambunctious teenager, back in the 1950s or 60s. He is followed by a young male assistant, who carries a black leather binder thick as a dictionary. The assistant is long-faced, with a mop of dark curly hair, and stands a full head taller than his boss. Young Ae titters involuntarily because when they come in through the door it looks as if the assistant's head is levitating above the lawyer. No one cares about the tittering.

The lawyer sits down and begins reading from the will. No one is surprised by the huge sum of money and property that the dead woman has amassed from years of real estate dealings. Of course there is no mention of her ex-husband, but there is also no mention of her siblings who still live in Korea. There is mention of various Buddhist temples though, mostly in California and two in Korea. They get rather generous endowments and Young Ae and her husband feel their inheritance being diced away, but there is still enough left. Finally, the lawyer reads the sentences about the four sons. They receive the remainder of the still sizeable estate, to be divided perfectly equally, between all four men.

THE BOWL AND THE PISTIL

When Bettie was a puppy, she was afraid of the doorbell. She would bolt from wherever she was, however comfortably she had positioned her body, run up to the door of our apartment and point herself at it, curl her lips and bark continuously in a high pitch she saved just for the doorbell. Bradley and I would pry her away but it was difficult work and shockingly so, because Bettie weighed just 16 pounds. But she would make herself as still and dense as a very small wrought-iron object. The fur on the back of her neck rose up and out in spikes, and it is a miracle to see the soft waves of an Irish Setter, the only obvious portion of her totally illegible mutt self, turn poker-straight. Because she was so loud and because the walls of our building are not too thick, I feigned frustration but secretly, I loved to watch Bettie get crazy at the doorbell because the transformed fur was beautiful to look at, and even more beautiful to touch: the wonder of how a soft warm nestling becomes shards and needles through just the focused exertion of small muscles suffused with anxiety. For Bradley it was only a nuisance and that reaction was appropriate. It truly was a terrible nuisance, but I also felt like I understood where she was coming from; the doorbell scares me, too.

But Bettie is no longer afraid of the doorbell, and not because we hired a trainer or a dog psychologist. Around the time she was getting to be a year old, I started to answer and place anonymous sex ads on Craigslist. The ads I answer don't vary too much. Mostly they tend to ask for some sort of servitude, phrased in a vaguely homophobic and openly misogynistic way: "seeking cocksucking bitch," "Need Bitch With Boy Pussy." I answer these ads because experience taught me that the violence of the language is an oversized shirt under which a mild boy sits with a hard-on. In my own invitations for these gentle assholes I describe myself as "cocksucking bitch," "Bitch With Tight Boy Pussy" or more rarely because it doesn't seem as effective in tempting horny guys, "Queer With Quivering Boy Pussy." Even when you are horny sometimes you feel like staying political. I draw the line at calling myself a "bottom" because I don't believe in gay labels. I'm a white boy with very even features and soft wavy hair cut in a good homosexual haircut just this side of preppy, and my septum is pierced: from it hangs a golden semicircle ornament with the slightest tribalistic flourish.

In our living room there are two sofas: a small pretty one that barely sits two but accommodates three thin people, and a huge ugly brown leather thing. The pretty sofa, ordered from a designy catalogue, is velvet that is in fact some kind of stain-resistant polyester. But it's a great shade of marigold that goes to a just discernible shade of orange when you put some pressure on it. But it is uncomfortable. The other sofa is overstuffed and gleaming, but in fact quite soft to sit on. It was bought at a vintage furniture store just a few blocks away from our home and Bradley and I carried it home together by ourselves. It was bought at my insistence: I thought it so spectacularly ugly. It was one of the many hopelessly gay male things I commit every day. This sofa is a porn 'stache. But the two of them stand companionably next to each other.

In fact, in our home there are two or three of every piece of furniture, all unmatching. Every piece was bought but each has an idiosyncratic aura of being inherited through lineage or gifted with affection. There is a large mid-century tea-table of caramel oak with caramel brass fittings whose contrastingly prissy minimalist design and ridiculous size would have been perfect in a Connecticut den, cheesy like an early episode of *Mad Men*. This thing we shoved to the edge of the room, underneath a fixture of shelves made of thick industrial-grade wire and featherweight metal slats, into which we shoved books in no order whatsoever. The heavier art books went on and under the tea-table so it looked as if the books and the wall shelves melted together onto the floor. The table we used to for coffee and TV dinners is actually a surfboard pegged with four pretty metal antique chair legs. The glossy polyurethane of the surfboard was proudly scarred with scuffs of use, and whether the artisan forged them to give a sufficiently rugged masculine patina, we don't know, and of course it doesn't really matter; in general, we care little for authenticity in big showy things. The fin of the table (surfboard) is hung with our keys and some-times my unhooked earrings and long pendant necklaces. All our rooms, including the bathroom, overflow with furniture and knick-knacks. Sometimes it seems to me that the oozing clutter of our home is the only thing pre-venting Bradley from catching on to the smell or feeling of other men. Bettie knows everything. After the unlucky first ten guys who had to endure her growls and barks to get their cocks in my mouth or ass, she got used to the regular rotation of males who were not me or Bradley. I think she accepted strange male smells as part of the air of the city itself. In sum: our girl stopped barking so hard at strange men.

My laptop is open and the email account that I use only for sex indicates a new message from Craigslist. My ad (today I was feeling political so my Boy Pussy was not Tight but Assenting) has been answered and there is a guy's offer to come over. The guy says he doesn't live too far from me and would walk over but because he's walking, would I mind waiting fifteen minutes. I think: fifteen minutes' worth of walking doesn't sound close to me but I like that he actually used the phrase "would you mind waiting" in the email. It's weirdly formal, neither the nervously icy voice of really repressed and closeted guys nor the overly friendly voice of guys trying to per-form casual heterosexuality.

My response contains my usual request to meet at a café two blocks from my house: if he matches his face pic and we like each other, we will go back to my house. The guy's response to my response: "Sounds good. See you there in twelve minutes." The number twelve is spelled out. Bettie follows me as the computer is closed and clothing is gathered to put directly over my naked body: a vintage boiler suit in navy cotton, on its back a yellow silkscreen cracking into powder at the edges: a cartoon of a Ford Thunderbird with long batting lashes over its front windshield and over that image, in curly script: "GINA'S AUTO BODY." On the front left pocket is a white patch embroidered in red: "Rod." Buttoned up from crotch to three buttons from the top, it reveals short, straight blond hairs growing out of my sternum and the hollow of my neck. Bettie gets a nuzzle before the door closes behind me.

At the café, the guy is already there even though my departure was timed exactly to set my arrival at ten minutes from the moment my laptop was closed. He stretches in his seat a little. When he puts his hands behind his head, you can see thick tufts of long black armpit hair falling from the hems of his t-shirt sleeve. I'm certainly attracted; I like it when there is a touch of a beast, or at least unkempt wild messiness, on a man who has a traditionally handsome face. His face looks exactly like his face pic, even his hair, parted and styled the same, the same length too, as if he had taken the pic as he attached it to the email. I'm glad because I know I look exactly like my face pic. Before him a steaming paper cup, and on a pile of paper napkins, half of a scone. This café is famous for their vegan scones, which are the size of a saucer and thick as a bible, loaded with both nutritious nuts and twigs and sugar (beet sugar, say the cards at the cake case). He's got one with bitter chocolate chips, and he's gotten some on his mouth, which he wipes with the back of his hand. Wearing plain black jeans and a dark blue Belle & Sebastian t-shirt, he's not reading anything, not pretending to do anything except drink his coffee or tea and eat his big ass scone, leisurely, long legs now folded awkwardly under a tiny square table. I imagine him knocking it over with his knees when he gets up. We see each other and I wave first. He waves back, and as I approach him he does get up from the table; he doesn't knock the table over. He's not pulling the chair out for me or anything, but he remains standing until I pull it out myself and sit down.

"Hi."

"Hey."

Pleased, I smile at him and think he smiles back but I'm not sure. Maybe it's the way his jaw is set, or maybe his mouth, but I'm pretty sure he's not smiling. But the look on his face is definitely pleased, even though from a different angle, it could look as though he is scowling. He opens his mouth and takes a huge bite that halves the half scone.

"I got you a coffee, but maybe you don't drink coffee. Do you want a tea instead or something?"

Indeed, the paper cup is filled to the rim. "Oh, that's nice of you. Thanks, but I'd better not...you know, if we do stuff, caffeine might not be the best thing right before." Saying this feels weird but he nods as if it's a totally natural thing.

"Sure, yeah." He picks up the cup and takes a slurpy sip. "I like this place. I've never been here before. I'll have to remember it, the baked stuff seems really good."

"Are you vegan?"

"Yeah, or I try to be as much as possible. I like sweets but I'm really not into bone char."

I have no idea what he's talking about but don't ask because small talk is not really what I am feeling right now, but at the same time, this doesn't feel like typical pre-sex small talk either: no vibrating urgency underneath the boring short words.

"Are you a fan of Belle & Sebastian?"

"What? Oh yeah, they're good, I think. This is actually my wife's shirt. But I like them, yeah. They're kind of like, vegan music."

"Ha, right." I watch him finish off the scone. "Well, do you still feel like it?"

He chews and nods. "Yeah. Definitely. Let's go."

Bettie looks up at the guy when we walk in and making eye contact, starts wagging her tail, metronome on high tempo. The guy reaches down and scratches her head with his knuckles.

"Aww, what a cutie. Look, his feet are in third position, like ballet. Hey, buddy."

"He usually barks at strangers." I don't feel like correcting the guy about Bettie's gender; I'm too lazy today for extra words. But something makes me keep talking rather than just pull him into the bedroom. "Do you have a dog?"

"Yeah. One dog, no kids."

"I guess he just likes you, or your dog." I reach over and feel the middle of his chest with my fingertips. "I like you too."

He stops scratching Bettie.

"Me, too."

In the moments taken up with trying to decide whether I should or can kiss him, he says, "Do you want to go to your room or shall we stay here?"

I take his hand and walk him hand-in-hand to the bedroom. I unbutton my jumpsuit and step out of it, feeling like a molting snake. I am naked before him and the windows are open. The early summer breeze ruffles all the thin hairs on my body. I want the guy to come over and touch me in a way to create soft electricity between my skin and body hair. That desire makes a tingle in my nipples, glittery and vague. They feel suddenly very heavy and hurt a little. The guy doesn't make a move but stands at the edge of the bed and looks me up and down. He sits and kicks off his shoes, then takes off white socks. His penis pokes out of the split fly of plaid boxer shorts. The head of his penis is rather pointed, very red and swollen, a honey-drop of precum clinging like dew at the piss slit. He pulls off his underwear, tossing it, making a pile of his shoes, socks, pants. He sits on the edge of the bed and absent-mindedly begins masturbating. His penis is not big, but it looks very hard. With a thumb and two fingers, he jacks it. His balls, however, are huge: they droop in their long smooth ball-sac, resting against the inside of his thighs. They wriggle a little, like living things in dark pink thick veiny skin.

His legs are loosely spread, and with my whole body I pry them open to an uncomfortable angle, but he doesn't show any sign of discomfort. I take him in my mouth and suck. There is a real pleasurable feeling; he isn't testing my gag reflex so it doesn't feel like pornography, but I roll the thing around in my mouth and it is indeed really hard. It could be Viagara but the hardness is not so insistent as it is tensile. It's not like warm metal; it's like hard candy that takes forever to lick down. So I lick and suck and roll. It keeps spraying precum on my tongue, into the crevices of my teeth. Spit and precum drip down from my mouth.

I look up and he is looking down at me. His gaze is focused but not intense, amused but not smug. He reaches over and ruffles my hair like you would a dog. I see that he is still wearing his t-shirt.

I stop sucking for a bit and with a wet drooling mouth, say, "Will you take that off?"

"Yup." He does. I kiss his belly, up to his chest, hard nipples, all hairless. I can smell a deep funk of his armpits, and big black bushy armpit hair that tufts wildly out into the outer corners of his chest. I kiss his mouth, insert my tongue and he kisses me back.

We lay on the bed, both of us on our sides. With his knuckle the guy begins rubbing the little rounded ridge of bone just above the root of my penis. It isn't really rubbing—more like kneading, more like he's trying to pulverize my pubic bone in small increments. His knuckles have sparse straight dark hair; it's pretty. His hand is big so it's only two fingers digging into me, making that small edge of bone feel curved and smooth, curvier and smoother than it is in reality. I want to say it made my whole body feel like a vagina, except I had an erection. But it does make me feel like a vagina, because while I'm getting harder, I have no desire to jerk off or pay attention to my penis at all. He rubs me in a way that reminds me of times when I would lay on our velvet sofa, back and ankles at each horizontal end, writing stuff with my laptop balanced over my pubic bone. Sometimes, the low hum of the computer would vibrate my pubic bone in a pleasurable way.

Our fucking feels clean. When he puts his cockhead against my asshole and pushes in, I don't feel split apart or like I'm made of liquid. Instead, I feel like myself, like I can't escape myself even by orgasm. His penis rocks me in a probing, curious pattern. It feels like a sound—a sound that is clear, a bit blaring and beautiful. It could be music, music made by something metal (A trumpet? A Hare Krishna's tapping an empty metal rice bowl?), music that is calmly defiant of any tunefulness, resistant to remembering or humming. He fucks me from behind, and when I try to push back into him or to participate in the rhythm of his thrusts, he grabs my waist and holds me in the place that he likes. Still in the middle of his fucking me, my penis ejaculates. From my position, I bow my head and catch some of my own jizz spraying onto my chest hair and on the sheets under me. At the end of that tunnel of my body being fucked are his balls, still hanging and slapping my ass but moving closer to his own body. He comes a little later. He pulls out and still upside down, I could see him roll the condom away from his still hard cock and tie its lip into a nice tidy knot; I think of me tying the same knot in Bettie's poop bag.

I start to get up but he mutters a quiet "Uh-uh" and keeps me in place. Holding the knotted condom in his left hand, he sticks his middle finger into me and begins to fuck me again. He sticks his index finger in too and rubs my prostate until I become hard again. He fucks me like this for a few minutes, until I go soft. I don't ejaculate again but it feels good.

"Where shall I throw this away?" he asks. We are still naked. He's standing at the foot of the bed, me still on my stomach.

"In the trash in the bathroom?" I would take out the trash when he'd gone.

After the condom is disposed, we sit next to each other at the foot of the bed, neither of us reaching for our clothes.

"What is your wife like?" I ask.

"She's a dancer. I mean, she used to be a dancer. She's in graduate school now."

"For dance?"

"No, for English."

"Do you have a picture of her?"

To my surprise, he doesn't act embarrassed or awkward. There's silence but he walks over to his pile of clothes and pulls out a brown leather wallet, obscenely stuffed. It's so full of stuff its shape is no longer square but a sphere. Acting as if showing a photo of his wife to an anonymous sex partner were the most socially natural thing, he shuffles through the wallet, which is filled with business cards, punch cards for wine shops, coffee places, movie tickets, dry cleaning tickets, BART tickets, bus transfers, credit card receipts, bank receipts, and interspersed between all that junk, intervals of rolled and folded up cash. I keep thinking shit was going to fall out and then there would be a madcap scramble for funfetti, but amazingly, that doesn't happen. Finally he unearths a folded-up photo about twice the length of a playing card. In the photo is an Asian woman, maybe Native American, from the top of her head to four breast bones' length of her chest. Four is an exact number in this case because you could see the bones through her skin. She has a long, humorless face and an angular long nose. Her long black hair is pushed back without a part and flows behind her, so that no strand of hair interrupts her bare shoulders. She looks straight into the camera with the inky black eyes of a cute doll, but unsmiling with neither eyes nor mouth. Her skin isn't silky smooth; you could see all the striations of the muscles on her shoulders and arms, and her neck is kind of thick; she's kind of beautiful, but not exactly pretty.

"She's pretty," I lie. The guy shrugs, and we both continue looking at the picture on his lap. Feeling brave, I venture: "She looks kind of like a delicate man, though."

The guy makes an inquisitive shape with his mouth that isn't attractive. "You think so? I guess, maybe. I never noticed it before."

"Maybe that's why you're attracted to her."

He looks up from the photo at me. "Because I have sex with men?"

"Yeah."

His mouth becomes that unattractive shape again. I think maybe he'll start to spout some boring shit, like "Oh no, that's just to get off, I'm really in love with my wife." Instead, the guy says: "Yeah, maybe. It's probably not that important, though."

He folds up the photo and sticks it gently back into his wallet. I feel small and petty.

"What do you do," I ask.

"I'm an actor."

"Oh wow. Are you on stage or TV or film? Would I have seen you in anything?"

"Mainly stage. But you wouldn't have seen me in anything. I haven't worked in a while. I just do odd jobs for the time being." He smiles a big unrepressed smile.

His teeth are actor's teeth: big, white, perfectly square. Teeth like Chiclets or expensive bathroom tiles. They look capped, which I usually find kind of gross but on this guy, they look beautiful. The teeth leap when he smiles. The smile pushes his chin down into his neck, making weird wrinkles and rendering him almost chinless. But that makes him look a little charming. I have a fucked-up front tooth from a fight in a gay bar last year. It was knocked out by a drunk straight guy who thought (correctly) that I had insulted his girlfriend. But the straight guy was wearing some kind of ring that also chipped the tooth as well as knocking it out. They were able to save the tooth and stick it back in, but the ring-chip made it look like the end of a chisel. Bradley really thinks I should get it capped but I refuse, because I think of myself as beyond conventional vanity and like I said, I like worn things, even if that thing is a part of my body. But seeing this guy smile his big, chin-disappearing smile makes me self-conscious about the fucked-up tooth and I feel a little ugly. But not really.

I watch the guy put his clothes back on. He puts on his sneakers last—they're Vans Era lace-ups in black cotton, worn and old and dirty. I notice for the first time a hole in his right shoe, where his big toe sticks out. It makes him look a bit like a bum.

He notices me looking at his foot and shrugs and grins. "Yeah, it makes me kind of look like a bum, but they're my favorite, so Oh Well, you know? My right foot is bigger than my left, and I can't do anything about that, you know?"

I nod and walk him to the door. Bettie is sleeping on the velvet sofa, her dainty body stretched out, louche. She stirs at bit and opens her eyes but she's bored by us, and closes them again. We don't talk about hooking up again, and I can feel that neither of us are sure we want to, even though we both had a good time. I want to give him something. I've always wanted to be the kind of person who gives clothes away; they do it in movies and novels, but they are always girls. And this gesture, part of a very small group of gestures, feels right only when done by girls; there's something very stupid about a guy handing over jeans or a t-shirt to another guy as a gesture. The clothes being gifted have to be dresses, or very tight jeans that slice you down the middle. I think it's something about intimacy, or relatedly, handing over a completed version of yourself, part and parcel, in one piece of clothing. I've always wanted to be this kind of person but one, I am not a girl, and two, I am very selfish. When Bradley and I moved in together one of the big rules I made was not sharing clothes, even though we are roughly the same size. But with this guy, I want to give him one of my t-shirts. It is itself a shirt that didn't originally belong to me. One summer in high school I had a part-time job painting houses. I showed up for the first day of work dumbly in a dumb Lacoste polo. My boss, a forty-one year old man whose face had already gone much older due to all his time spent outside, but whose body was long-boned and ageless, laughed at me and dug up an old t-shirt out of his car trunk, balled it up, and tossed it to me. It might have been a concert t-shirt at one time but by then it had faded into gibberish. Besides, he (or someone he knew) had tie-dyed it so its greying white surface was covered with creamsicle orange and antifreeze blue. I wore the shirt all summer and it became splattered with white, pale yellow, violet-grey. I imagine offering this guy this shirt and him in turn offering to trade his wife's Belle & Sebastian. But as a gesture, it would be better if we did this on the street, in public, instead of this fluid privacy. But he doesn't look like the kind of guy who would give away his wife's clothes, even if he's wearing them. I imagine this guy putting my shirt on: it would stretch pretty tight instead of hanging sack-like as it does on my own torso. I think of it sitting in my drawer that sits flush against Bradley's. It's folded up into a very small, tight square. I imagine going to get it, giving it to him, a costume for a character he might play.

The guy mentioned earlier that he's Korean American; Bradley's parents are Japanese American. Bradley is one of the native born-and-bred San Franciscans, not sad immigrants from Iowa like me. His dad was even interned with his parents at Topaz. It always makes me sad and a little guilty that I think of topaz the stone when I think about Topaz the internment camp but I can't help it; the history of oppression suffered and overcome in Bradley's genealogy adds to his beauty. Bradley is beautiful and sexy but his beauty and sexiness have become smooth and crystalline—so many pretty, hard facets that refract everything, ethereal and material, that touches it. When I look at him I feel touched, like I want to put him behind glass where he won't get dusty or chipped.

BONNY, BLYTHE, GOOD, AND GAY

Sex at pre-dawn, anytime between 4:00 and 5:30 am, when the sparrows are barking, makes you feel simultaneously dazed and alert, like you've had your internal organs scooped out and replaced with something crystalline but combustible, all corners and catching light, fluorescent or pastel, going to pieces and warmth. It hurts because the edges are sharp and the lining of your human cavity is still soft, warm and damp, but it makes you feel completely empty and hollow, in a good way. And because it was dawn, and outside the sparrows had begun barking for real for a while now, from a distance, Donny, a.k.a. Sunday's Child, and Young Ae looked together like a pale long-winged bird bisected by a vertical rectangle of hot solid pink. The funny thing is, Donny himself had an urgent feeling that he was creating this picture with Young Ae. Eating her vagina made him have the same feeling he had when as a five year old, he ate a triple-scoop cone of Neapolitan ice cream and then puked it all over himself, on his cute striped t-shirt, on the concrete at his feet as he stood between his solid parents. That is how they all discovered his lactose intolerance, but Donny never forgot that taste of the unbearably sweet ice cream, strawberry, chocolate, and vanilla, all swirled with his own bile that made it even more sweet as it filled the small wet cavity of his mouth and spewed out into the big world outside, despite the best efforts of his small wet teeth to hold it all in.

He buzzed at her labia for a spell, mostly out of boredom with himself making a wet sound of tiny sucks of air, and as he felt her buttock spasm in his grip, he buzzed some more. This made him think about the sound of buzzing, how sometimes it was indistinguishable from the sound of humming. In his brain were the words "hum" and "hmmm" and "buzz" and how they all produced the same family of sounds. This made him remember how he and Young Ae met: fighting over a vinyl single of "Lemon Incest." They were at a record store close to Young Ae's house but far from his own. He was in the neighborhood taking a meeting with a potential booker who had not been impressed with him at all. The booker was a young-looking person in their early thirties, hair heavy with blondness, from the Midwest, with a bland turgid plumpness that had a thick layer of sheen gathered from a work life spent on both coasts. When the booker saw him at the booth where he was already waiting, they had acted all excited, which struck him as ridiculous; they'd already met casually several times. Although Donny didn't think he looked different from any other average black man in his thirties, he thought to himself: Oh ya, you're responding to my 6 foot-6 Viking-meets-Shaka Zulu vibes, huh? As the meeting progressed, he could not only sense the booker's enthusiasm deflate, they went out of their way to indicate their disappointment. Of course, they were not explicit about why they were disappointed by him, and of course in Donny's mind he produced a lot of reasons why they were. The only thing they were explicit about was his atheism.

"From a development standpoint, I'm not sure that atheism is the strongest lead for you. You want to call yourself 'Blak Mass,' even. You seem insistent upon that being the only lead," they said as they picked at their burger. They had ordered a hamburger, rare, and when it arrived, sitting languidly on expensive brioche bun amid dollhouse pickles in exotic shapes and colors, they cleaved it determinedly in half. They picked up one half and took a small bite and not a bite more. The blood of the burger eventually made a pretty, ruby-colored pool that made the whole thing soggy and officially inedible.

"Well, yeah, it is," he answered.

"So I'm not sure what, if anything, I can do for you. I'm totally interested in idiosyncratic musicians, but I'm also interested in taking them out of the niche into a more mainstream realm. Do you even want that?"

"Yeah, I think I do."

"Well, you have to do more than think you do. You have to know. You have to want it, you know. I don't have to tell you about how competitive and cutthroat this business is."

"Sure."

After the meeting, Donny was filled with a feeling that had become very familiar to him: a mix of moral rectitude, artistic righteousness, and dejection. Holding this feeling close, rocking it nicely, he walked a few blocks to the record store, which was the basement flat of an otherwise nondescript and rather ugly townhouse in which Donny always presumed lived not a gang of young people sharing rent but some never-married old-timer who had lived in the neighborhood all their adult lives. Because of the dinginess of the face of the house, the store also appeared dingy from the outside. But once you stepped off the awkward concrete steps, and pushed open the frail door with its sad busted cat-door, you were already welcomed by a fresh, cold professionalism. The basement looked as though it had been whitewashed twice or even thrice. The white walls and floors had a particular whiteness that was totally opaque: it was the color of air conditioning. The two rows of bins were similarly whitewashed, and although it had to be wood, it felt and looked cold as marble for 19th Century Italians. One row of records stood between the other and a wall that held display shelves for especially rare items, the cash register, and a listening station, creating two very narrow aisles that led almost flush up against the back door of the room, which was always closed. The aisles were such that once one reached the end of one row of record browsing, one couldn't simply loop into the other side of the bin as in a supermarket, but rather, had to retrace one's steps back.

That day, the store was empty but for a plump cashier Donny didn't recognize, and an Asian woman about his age who was absent-mindedly thumbing through records. The shopper was Young Ae; to Donny, she looked irresistible. Flipping through the records with the quickness of an aficionado, she nevertheless would let fat stacks of records fall between, unpicked, while picking through others one by one with care and finickiness, seemingly randomly. She shopped with her right hand, while her left was held mid-air in a loose, expectant grip. Around her left forearm was the looped handle of a thick, mottled-purple dog leash. To Donny's eyes, the loop of leash looked like a bracelet pretending to be a cartoon snake pretending to be a bungee cord used to secure heavy stuff to cars. At the other end of the leash, which was pulled tight to its max, was a medium-sized dog. It was clearly a mutt, but as it moved its gleaming black snout obsessively around the white floor, flashes of Beagle and Golden Retriever phased in and out of its surface. The dog was clearly dividing its attention in equal amounts to the smells of the shop and the attention of its owner. As soon as Donny entered the store, it looked up sharply at his face and began barking, loud, short, machine-gun fire barks in time to its wildly wagging bushy tail.

"Marilyn. Quiet. Quiet," said Young Ae.

And like magic, the dog closed its mouth on its bark and stared up into the eyes of its owner with the air of not acquiescence but inquiry. The owner had spoken the words loudly and in a voice devoid of any feeling—not anger, not frustration or fluster. She jerked the leash towards her as she spoke, and stared down at her dog with a furrowed brow. Donny couldn't tell whether the expression was angry or not. Her face had become flushed bright red. As she turned to snap the leash, he saw that she was pregnant. As the dog quieted, she looked at Donny.

"I'm so sorry. I have no idea to this day why she barks at someone and not at others. I don't think it's necessarily a bad feeling, at least for her. But still, sorry."

"It's all good," he replied, and went to the other aisle as Marilyn's eyes followed him with now an unmistakable look of genuine interest. Donny began to pick through the records, although not with his usual vigor and diligence. There was a triangulation of interest: the focused one of Marilyn to Donny, a pretend-nonchalant sneaking of glances from Donny to Young Ae, and the slightly addled one of Young Ae, who kept on flipping through records while keeping an eye on Marilyn, whose expressive black lips sometimes went into sine waves of very low rumbling as if wanting to bark, but holding it back. The triangulated curiosity radiated low vibrations that predictably, only Marilyn could feel. Between stolen glances, Donny earnestly looked for records. All the records were used, and every one, even those with ratted sleeves, was held in transparent plastic casing. Having spent one afternoon going through literally all the records in the store, Donny knew that not all deserved the casing (Yet another dog-eared copy of Fleetwood Mac *Rumors*?) but he enjoyed the plastic's slippery texture. Unlike Young Ae, he went through the records one by one.

As Blak Mass (as he was known then), Donny was a rapper. But as Donny Larsson, he taught electrical engineering at one of the state universities in the area, and coding at a community college; both were part-time lectureships. He thought of himself more a rapper than "teacher" although if pressed, he thought of himself more as a poet who was good at fixing sounds. The phrase "fixing sounds" always had air quotes when he thought them. He never described himself as "a poet who was good at fixing sounds" because it sounded so pretentious. He would never even say it to his parents, and they were people with some laudable pretensions—his given, legal name was Duke Donald Larsson. He had had some local success, although "success" was probably an overstatement. There were a few shows at some small but definitely buzzworthy venues, and nice write-ups from local but influential critics followed. He had put together a reasonably successful EP that he released online, downloadable for free. But his audience seemed to be mainly young white people, college-age or immediately post-college, and that was not an audience he particularly respected nor craved. He felt like the state university was on the verge of offering him something full-time, and more and more, that felt more like something.

As he flipped through the "World Music" section, he wondered if the unimpressed booker was right, if he were in fact wrong to cling so hard to his moniker. He was an atheist, and an atheist poet. Disgust with not only organized religion but the very idea of any god was not just the result of a long intellectual and emotional process, it was now his artistic inspiration; atheist art was non-negotiable. But perhaps he could come up with a moniker that was a little less obvious, less religious or threatening? "Blak Sunday?" "Sunday's Child?" Or he could just go by what the kids used to call him in elementary school: Donald Duke. They had simply reversed his first and middle names, hadn't even bothered to change "Duke" to "Duck" because, obviously. He had really hated his parents then. Not so now, since as an adult, he rarely went by Donald and never by Duke, and always as Donny. He laughed to himself though to imagine swaggering as "Donald Duke" or "Duke Donald" or "Duke Don." He imagined that booker probably would have been happy with the third.

Donny pulled out a record that had been stuck in the stacks on its corner point; the song was "Lemon Incest" by Serge and Charlotte Gainsbourg. He knew what the song was and was repelled by the ugly cover image—an old white man, half-naked and pressing the profile of his fresh daughter—but curious about what it sounded like. He was drawn to the idea of finding a good sound out of such an ugly thing. Donny's artistic practice was: he wrote a poem, then found a small tab of sound, usually skimmed from an existing, bigger soundtrack, and around this one tab of sound (sometimes two) he would build some beats. He took the record over to the listening station and put it on. The song was cheap-sounding: the baby-breathy vocal of the girl and the signature song-chant of the gravelly man was cheap, and the blubbery tone of the generic 80s synth sounded cheap in the other way. The record was a single, so having listened to the title song, he turned the thing over to listen to the B-side, which was called "Hmm hmm hmm." This song was not much more musically interesting, but Donny found a tab of sound in it: the chorus was a male voice singing "Hmm hmm hmm," and the beginning of the third "hmm" had an unexpected upward movement that he dug instantly. It sounded like a simple intake of breath, but the gulping turned that breath immediately into a weird musical note.

As he still had the headphones on, he didn't feel Young Ae move towards him. But before the tap on his shoulder, he felt Marilyn's soft fur brush against his leg. He lifted the headphones off and turned to face her.

"I was going to buy that record," she said. Without the "Marilyn Quiet" furrow, her face was indisputably lovely to Donny.

"But you put it back."

"I turned it when I put it back so I could come back to it, but I think I forgot."

"Sorry, but I'm going to get it."

Young Ae looked as if about to pout, but the pre-expression dissolved. Still impassive, she said, "That's not really fair. I saw it first, I wanted it first. But I suppose you are right."

"Well, you're right too. Look, I don't even really want it. All I really want to do is take it home, sample a sound from it and work with it some. But I could give it to you after I'm done."

"You would do that? That would be nice of you."

"It's nothing."

"I'll pay for it of course."

"Nope. Then it wouldn't be a gift. It's for my work, and I can write it off on my taxes."

Young Ae looked at him.

"$7.00?"

"Why not?"

Donny looked down at Marilyn. She was sitting and looking up at him. Her eyes were very, very dark and her tail was wagging, thumping floor in a slow but regular rhythm. He thought what that sound might be like amplified into a beat.

"OK, then. Thank you. It's sweet of you."

"You're welcome."

"What do you do?"

"I'm a musician. I'm a rapper. A producer." He felt dumb as the words came out, even though in reality they sounded quite swaggering.

"You're going to rap to that?"

"Just the B-side. And just a small part of it. I'm more like...a poet good at fixing sound. You know?"

"I think so. Maybe?"

He noticed that she had a record in her hand and peered over to get a better look. It was a brilliant, seductive shade of dark green that formed a thick border around a smaller black-and white-image in the center. In the photograph, four men with shaggy, dry-looking hair were standing tightly together, all legs apart and tangled, torsos bent in poses that looked half balletic and half guitar-rock posturing. The photograph wasn't very well exposed, so the men, against the stark white backdrop, looked like pieces of Stonehenge. In elegant silver typeface at the top of the album were the words "V LEN." The middle letters were obscured by Young Ae's thin arm but Donny knew what they were.

"Are you a big Van Halen fan?"

"No. I don't even really know what they sound like. They're heavy metal? Are they good?"

"Well, nah. But the lead singer, David Lee Roth, he's I think...interesting. Why are you getting it if you don't know what it sounds like?"

"I don't know. Why not. Take a chance. I like the image. The silver and the dark green, look really beautiful together. It feels like buying a giant emerald."

She held up the thing as he looked closer.

"And the title is appropriate. Like a prophecy," he said.

"Huh?"

Donny pointed to the title. "*Women and Children First*."

"Oh, right." She patted her belly without affection. "I didn't even notice that. Well, hopefully not a prophesy. That would mean I'm going on a sinking ship." She smiled.

He smiled back. "Wrong word, I used." Nimbly, he took the record from her with two fingers and thumb. "Let me get that."

"Oh no, I couldn't."

"Come on. $4.00."

"OK. Thank you. Again."

"You're very welcome. Wait. Are you leaving now?"

"Yes. I really should get back home. I've been wandering around for a while and this girl is quite tired, I think."

"Well, give me your number. How else am I going to get the album to you? As a gift."

So she gave him her number, and they began a friendship that eventually found a sexual component as well. Young Ae orgasmed as Donny squeezed a butt cheek with one hand and circled a hard nipple with the palm of the other. He was imagining Young Ae's face as a flipbook of expressions, each page looking identical but in fact conveying a subtly different emotion which only became legible upon expert flipping. He thought: I wonder if she is not herself right now, or is she most herself? After she finished coming, Young Ae slid down off the edge of the bed onto the floor next to Donny. Donny had an overwhelming desire to fuck her immediately, to put his penis into that wet, raw, happy amber zone. But she had given birth just a few weeks before, and he knew—abstractly and viscerally—that she was not up for fucking. So he sat upright next to her and spread his legs out, settling into a comfortable position. He looked down, spat a long, thick dribble of spit onto his hard cock and began masturbating. Young Ae put her head on his shoulder, and he moved his head slightly to fit snugly against hers. He jacked off hard and fast until he, too, came, spurting thick but slow wads of sperm onto his belly and pubic area.

Young Ae's husband, who was at home with the baby and Marilyn, was not calling her right then because Young Ae's walks, jaunts, wanderings and disappearances caused him no anxiety: he had a tender indifference towards her. But even if he were calling her, even if he were setting off the vibrations of Young Ae's tiny cell phone, she would not have known because the phone was not tucked into the back or front pocket of snug jeans where it would subtly shake her private patches of skin. Rather, it was tucked inside her handbag, but the handbag was not flush against her ribcage, where the tissue-thin lambskin would prove no barrier to the phone's vibrating her third or fourth rib; the handbag was on the floor next to the cliché pile of lacy underwear. But the other discarded clothes of the man and the woman were less gendered, all crumpled on the floor: whose soft jeans were these, and whose shirt was this made in black flexible stuff all over with bright red tropical flowers in full bloom or shy green buds?

LES CAUSEUSES

About a week before Lisa Marie contemplated suicide, she met Young Ae at the laundromat; it all began as a wet t-shirt contest and turned into a tropical mudslide. Lisa Marie had the kind of face that looked soft and fat when she was being sweet, and when she was mean, became all skull: why, even the Kewpie doll-dimple in her chin disappeared. She was an actress, and male directors liked her because while she had the face and body of a teenager just beginning to shed baby fat, she moved with the slow, elegant slovenliness of a cow. Straight or gay, male directors liked to linger over her in slow motion, whether in the editing room or their brains, to refashion Lisa Marie's actual morphological function as a time-lapse video of a child becoming a woman. Such glittery perversity was not wholly lost on female directors either but a lot of them just found her kind of sloppy or sullen—which they didn't mind because it was refreshing to encounter an actress who radiated indifference in the shape of pure laziness rather than *haute* boredom. So while Lisa Marie's slowness endeared her to most technicians and crafters of film, it was also the reason she didn't do well with casting directors or producers. Reliant on headshots, they flipped right past her, for still photography made her face break down into a puddle of something sticky and not very sweet. It's also why for the past ten years she had been playing a stream of sullen teenaged daughters of rotating generations of 40-year old beauties rotating into a career of playing mothers and lawyers.

When her eyes first set upon Young Ae, Lisa Marie was sitting on an out-of-order washing machine labeled K, her laundry divided up evenly and turning in machines J and L. The walls of her vagina were thumping slowly and evenly, in a way that made her feel as though all her gross thick blood-flesh were tiny, perfect grains of sand in a hacky sack, which made her grin like an idiot. She was wearing a tight white cotton T-shirt with dark blue ringers. On the front was an appliqué of a bashful yellow bunny with extravagant eyelashes sitting on the words "GUCCY" intricately embroidered with a very thin kind of rope in ivory tones. It was a fake Gucci shirt from the 1970s, made in Korea, and its label said so. The shirt fit tight (not only did the costumer take it in to make it hug Lisa Marie's body, she put in sneaky darts, shelving for her breasts, made from the leftover scraps of the shirt). The shirt was tucked into olive army pants from the 1960s that too was taken in to fit Lisa Marie snugly at her waist and crotch. The pants accentuated her rather narrow but very fleshy-fat-padded hips. She wore white athletic socks with dirty canvas sneakers in what could be pale blue or dirty white. All of this, except the socks, was the costume she wore on the set of a film she finished last week. She didn't make too much money on the job but they let her walk off with some of the clothes, which she liked very much.

"She looks like Eva Marie Saint, in *On the Waterfront*," Lisa Marie said, looking at Young Ae.

"She who?" Young Ae asked.

"She you. You look like Eva Marie Saint in *On the Waterfront*."

"That's a sweet thing to say, but you do know I don't look anything like her."

"Why don't you?"

"For a start, I'm Asian."

"I'm white and blond doesn't mean I look more like her than you do. I'm white and blond, you are Asian and brunette, and you truly look more like Eva Marie Saint than I. You're very beautiful."

"Thank you."

"You're welcome. Your dress is pretty too, and it looks even prettier on you. I can tell it's vintage."

"It is vintage, but it's technically not a dress—it's a sweater and skirt."

"Yeah but I think when you're wearing a skirt it's always nice to call it a dress even if it isn't technically a dress. For you, especially because the sweater and the dress work together to make something, you, pretty. I like how it is really modest but totally sexual."

"Sexual? I don't think that's true."

"It's not seductive, like, you're not trying to get people to look at you in a sexual or erotic way, but it's sexual because it makes you seem naked. Because the skirt comes down to your ankles but it has just enough pleats to let you move in it. And the sweater is high-necked but the sleeves are short and it is tight, so you can tell you're not wearing a bra. And it's all the color of honey. So actually, the dress is really very revealing."

"I have barely anything to reveal."

"I think you have plenty to reveal, and it might be nice if you revealed more."

"Oh come on. I feel so frightfully lean and male."

"Yeah, you are lean. But hardly male!"

"I've always been flat chested, and I had a baby last year, so my tits are in really bizarre shape—they are long and droopy from being sucked the hell out of by my child, but my nipples are still small and pointy."

"But I like your small and pointy nipples. They are cute, like little thumb tacks covered in plush."

"Are you hitting on me?"

"Maybe."

"I think technically you are hitting on me."

"Maybe, technically, I am."

"I'm not gay."

"Maybe I am."

"Are you?"

"Yeah, I am."

"You are silly."

"Yeah, I'm a silly kind of dyke. I became a lesbian because I find semen repulsive. I sucked a boy's penis once, when I was sixteen—he was sixteen too, another child actor—and he came in my mouth. Immediately I ran in the bathroom and spat it out into the sink because I hated the taste and feel of the stuff. Then I looked at it: it looked just like it tasted: rancid glue, grey, pus from a wound you need to drain in order to not die from infection, repugnant. I sucked his dick because being an actor, he was pretty, and his body was quite pretty as well, and I had nothing against dicks, personally. But tasting sperm really recast men in a whole new light. I just didn't like fucking them any more. I can appreciate the beauty of men, just like I can appreciate the beauty of women, but I prefer to suck the folds of labia than underneath foreskin or where foreskin used to be. That's how I became a lesbian. Am I talking too much?"

"Yes, but I like it. I like listening. But I like listening to you especially."

"Are you sure you're not gay?"

"Yes."

"I wish we could be friends."

"Why not? What is your name?"

"Lisa Marie. What is yours? And what is the name of your dog? She is so well-behaved. Look how she's just laying there curled up and so quiet by your feet."

"Usually she's crazy about investigating everything around her. I think it's because it's so hot today."

"She has a little pale pink petal in her nostril. It looks so cute, almost as if you stuck it in there yourself, for decoration, although I'm sure that must not be the case."

"It isn't. She loves to investigate, and today is so windy and weirdly humid it seems as though pollen and loose petals from trees were everywhere between the sidewalk and the airplanes zooming around above us. She was smelling hard at the root of a flower tree, and it got lodged in there. She does look so cute with it though, you are right. I can't believe it's still stuck there. I wish I had a camera."

"If you had a smartphone and had it with you."

"I do have one, but not with me. I suppose that makes the best incentive to carry it around at all times."

"Funny how you brought her but left your one year old at home!"

"Well, I have a husband. And honestly, it is less trouble to bring along a dog to do your non-delicates than a one-year old human. By the way, how did you guess my dog's gender? Most people think she's male. They're always greeting her saying stuff like 'What's up, Buddy?'"

"I should tell you that I have mystic vision for zeroing in on the obscured genitalia of dogs. I think most people assume that most dogs are male; I just assume that most animals are female."

"Her name is Marilyn. Mine is Young Ae."

"That is a very pretty name. I wish my name were Young Ae. I should have changed it to that, or something like that, but I'm sure if I did some people would be mad that some blond white girl chose an Asian name for herself, which is sad because I always felt some affinity towards Asian culture. I wish I looked less like me and more like you. My eyes are so ugly, they make my face look like a bullfrog and people say oh you have beautiful eyes, which is such bullshit. I wish I had clean, narrow eyes, or rather, clean narrow eye openings, I guess. Our eyeballs are probably the same size and certainly the same shape. And my hair is so dry and stringy, especially in this color. I wish it were like yours, glossy and black and cut in a tidy, steady, clean bob, parted on the side. White people, especially, white women, are so boring, don't you find?"

"But how would anyone know that you chose the name for yourself? I'm sure most people would just assume that you were part Korean (it's a Korean name; I'm Korean) rather than that you were…a…cultural appropriator?"

"Well, in my line of work people *would* ask where my name came from, and I would definitely be accused of being a cultural appropriator. I know plenty of Asian women with names like Jennifer or Tiffany or Laura. I don't know why a white girl can't go around her life with names like Ming-Na or Setsuko or Gong or Young Ae. A pretty name is a pretty name, don't you think? A pretty name shouldn't have a nationality."

"What do you do for a living?"

"Ha, I'm an actress."

"Really, you're an actress."

"Yes ma'am, I'm an actress."

"Would I have seen you in anything?"

"Well, probably, but you probably don't remember me. I was, like, a child actress and I'm still like a child actress because I am twenty-five and my specialty is sulky teenage daughters. And my special specialty is playing sulky teenage daughters of very thin, very pretty actresses in their 40s who are transitioning into playing mothers and lawyers. I think at some point, all actresses want is to be photographed beautifully so they can have a functional version of body dysmorphia. I wish I were a different kind of actress."

"What kind of actress do you want to be?"

"I want to be the kind of actress about whom people— you know, people in the industry, who've worked with me—say I am hard-working *and* talented. Isn't it horrible when you are talented, and you can glide by so you don't do anything and be an asshole? And just as horrible, too, to be so untalented you have to work your ass off and people look at what you did, shrug, and go 'hunnnhh.'"

"I wonder at your being an actress at all."

"Why?"

"Actors in general seem kind of dumb. Tell them to laugh, and they laugh. Tell them to cry, they cry."

"I see what you mean. I don't know, I am kind of dumb so maybe it fits."

"You don't seem dumb to me, but I don't know. Maybe I don't mean 'dumb' as in 'stupid,' but truly dumb, as in mute, like in the beautiful way of animals. They understand humans, and they can even speak. But not our language, so although they can say what they desire, they can never tell us what they desire. So it's more like they're not totally free."

"I just got déjà vu. But you're right. They're not free. I should say 'We're not free,' really, but I think I'm still in denial about the whole business. Mostly, I'm sick of feeling inferior to the characters I play. You know, I just did a movie with Robin Wright Penn. I don't know exactly how old she is but she must be edging toward her forties because they hired me to play her daughter. Actually, Robin Wright Penn does look like she's in her forties because she has a surprisingly large number of deep wrinkles around her eyes. Laugh lines, they are called, I guess. I hope she laughs a lot, because she is very beautiful and deserves a lot of laughter in her life. Anyway, I just finished playing her sulky 15-year old daughter and brought a book to the set, a serious book, William James, to read between takes. Not to show off but because I'm genuinely interested in philosophy. But while I was reading the book on set I felt like the biggest fraud. I had the sick feeling that I was actually just doing it to show off, to look intelligent, more intelligent than the other actresses or actors my age who show up on set gabbing on their cell phones. But I didn't feel more intelligent, I felt just as dumb. It's because the character I play, this dumb sulky girl, is smarter than I am. Or at least, she is more complicated than I am. I'm sick of being less complicated, more shallow, than the characters I play."

"You can't just quit being an actress I suppose."

"I could just quit. I'm young enough."

"You are. Young enough."

"But am I though? I'm 25. I was emancipated from my parents when I was 16 but I've never been to college. I've been acting since I was nine years old. I like to read but I couldn't repeat ideas to you in my own words. I'm not sure I can formulate any interesting ideas of my own and sure as hell, I can't write anything. I literally have no other skills. So what can I transition into? All I do is wonder: What kind of actress will I be in 2016? Will I turn into something wild and adult, or implode? There are a lot of girls who can't shake off the fat and roundness that look so irresistible on toddlers and children, then they get to be adults and their careers just end. Or they end up specializing in best friends, fat best friends, fat girls. Fat girls. Fat actresses. I feel like I'm already that close. Sometimes I want to kill myself."

"My husband says, 'I don't have feelings of wanting to kill myself, but I often want to never have been born.'"

"I don't know if I feel exactly that way. But that sounds cute."

"It's not cute to hear it from your husband, on a semi-regular basis. It's a drag."

"I'm glad you didn't tell me 'Oh no, don't say that' when I said I want to kill myself."

"Don't get me wrong though. I don't think that is a good way of feeling or thinking. It's just that you said *sometimes* you want to kill yourself. I think we all want to kill ourselves sometimes. It's about hanging on I guess."

"And it's better than sometimes wanting to kill someone."

"Absolutely. That's what I mean. People who want to kill themselves are better than people who want to kill other people."

"But is it OK to want to punch someone in the face?"

"Yes, that is OK."

"I often feel that way. But then I can never remember where my thumb is supposed to go. Do you? No, see, I don't either. Am I supposed to tuck my thumb in? Or am I supposed to wrap it around my knuckles to keep from breaking my thumb when I punch someone? I think you're supposed to keep it out, because if you tuck inside, then you might break your thumb with the force of your own fist? I don't know, any way you think about it, you'll probably break your thumb if you hit someone hard enough, right? I think it's the kind of thing that some boy, some boyfriend, is supposed to tell you about, but in my case, obviously, that doesn't work."

"I thought lesbians were supposed to be tough. So you should know that already, right?"

"Yeah, you're right! I should know already! I have a cheap antique ring with a ball of tangled brass noodles where a fat stone ought to be. It fits only on my ring finger on my right hand, and even then it's a little loose, but at least it goes on over my knuckle without getting stuck or slipping off. I got myself the ring to cure myself of an annoying habit. Instead of twirling my hair, I would turn the ring round and round on its finger using my thumb. Often, I'd keep the wrong side out so that when I made a fist, I could wrap my finger around the brass ball and transfer my warmth into it. It would help me remember that I'm a mammal and capable of radiating heat. But these moments of calming myself must have looked to other people like I was tense, getting ready for a street fight."

"Is your name really Lisa Marie? I mean, is that the name your parents gave you?"

"No, the name my parents gave me is Laura. But do you know how many Laura Rodgers there are in the industry? It's not just Actor Equity or Screen Actors' Guild: it's set designers, costume designers, drivers, stunts, editors, camera operators. There's a billion Laura Rodgerses *and* Laura Rogerses. So I became Lisa Marie Rodgers."

"Oh my god, I think there's a bee in my hair!"

"It's a wasp, actually. It's OK. Just now it climbed off and flew off."

"Are you sure?"

"Yes. It's gone. You're safe."

"A wasp? Why didn't I see it land? It was just at the end of my hair…"

"Oh, because it was in your hair when you came in. It was sitting kind of close to your ear."

"You mean it was sitting in my hair this whole time?"

"Yes."

"Why didn't you tell me? It could have stung me!"

"I wouldn't have let it hurt you. I was watching it the whole time. If it made a wrong move, I would have reached out and grabbed it myself. I would have let it sting me rather than hurt you."

Lisa Marie never became a big fat movie star, or a

serious actress who would star as Grushenka in a passion project of the film of *The Karamazov Brothers*, but neither did she grow fat, happily or in depression, become a mother or elementary school teacher or day care worker, nor did she for a long time to come, by her own hand or another's or accidentally, die.

ISABELLE ADJANI

Obviously, it is impossible that the genes of another girl can make it up into your body then climb into your ovaries. But at a moment, years later, Young Ae's son's face resembled not Young Ae's, not his father's, but that of Young Ae's best friend. Young Ae had not seen or talked to Ji Eun in years, but if she found out today that Ji Eun had died, she would blurt out that she had never and could never love another girl as much as she loved Ji Eun. Ji Eun was beautiful in a way that was ahead of her time. She had an unbearably narrow face that seemed to not have enough room to hold together black eyes that were black, not a metaphor for dark brown, but truly black, and puffy lips naturally the color of coral. Ji Eun's face would have been beautiful in any condition, but she had mild bulimia, and the waste it tolled upon her face made it look even more beautiful—translucent, the normal golden tone of her skin filtered a pale blue. The sadness of the waste outweighed the beauty for anyone who knew her. When Young Ae first saw her, she knew nothing about Ji Eun's eating disorder, so she felt no sadness in wondering, in admiration, how it was possible that this girl resembled so much a certain young French actress who was popular around the time she was born, the mid-late 1970s. This actress had a face of pointy placidness that stirred any inspiration of sexual desire in its beholder down to a coldness that felt refreshing, a stilled batter of something made mostly of sugar and dust. The French actress and Ji Eun were both a girl-shaped pile of loosely-packed white powder. Most of those who found Ji Eun beautiful were content to behold this weird powder-sculpture and leave it in peace. To Young Ae, Ji Eun gave an urge to crush her back into a storm of sweet dust. The French actress too had a narrow face, and eyes also set close in a way that just a centimeter or two closer to the bridge of her nose and she would have looked stupid but those crucial couple centimeters gave the actress a look of implacable seriousness that suited her very quiet intelligence. On the other hand, Young Ae thought with great affection that her best friend always looked a little stupid.

Both Young Ae and Ji Eun radiated softness, but Young Ae was tortured by a feeling, every day, of being a knife made out of calico and cotton stuffing, constantly trying to cut stuff harder than herself. With her angled, congenitally fatless face, Young Ae was arguably slightly more gorgeous than Ji Eun, but when people saw the two together they found Ji Eun to be the beautiful one, probably because Young Ae had a tendency to lecture, hands perpetually karate chopping in counterweight time to her massive verbiage as Ji Eun usually stood silently, slightly behind her. People used to men's ways of desiring women found her silence to be gentle and sweet, a welcoming passivity. But others were slightly frightened by it: it was like the silence of a blank-eyed dog, whose lips are slightly apart with just the teensy bud of the cutest pink tongue pushed out, and everyone knows that such a dog is ready to let out of that cute slimy lip either bark or yawn. Ji Eun rarely gave a pure bark but sometimes a bark came out in the middle of a yawn. This made people sit up and take notice before turning quickly away to forget that sound and the face from which it came. Dogs, on the other hand, tended to flock to her and loved her unconditionally. Marilyn would have died for her.

Both girls were student-dancers at the National Ballet Academy of Seoul. In springtime, the girls would go out for lunch immediately after class without bothering to change. Being ballet dancers, they loved simple gestures that got to be unnecessarily complicated, so they loved to pull on thick big men's sweaters over their thin rehearsal clothes for the bright sunlight of a cold Korean spring. On their sweat-glossed faces they only added a thick black line of pencil over the tops of their eyes. Ji Eun, handy with a pencil, on paper as well as on skin, a master of the perfectly sloped cat-eye, drew them on for her best friend before doing her own. And they switched to proper shoes: girlishly, they had bought identical knee-high suede boots, Young Ae's a deep forest green, Ji Eun's, a weird purple-oxblood. They looked like flower children regressing to chic Mod chicks.

One such springtime, the girls put on their eyes, boots, and sweaters, and were accosted by a group of high school thugs like flirtatious Nazis in dark, silver-buttoned uniforms. The silver buttons undone to reveal crisp white undershirts, they circled Young Ae and Ji Eun and began taunting them in a threatening but innocent way. Using rolled up notebooks and flat bamboo rulers, they poked at the girl's legs with short, musical jabs. They moved like infants and spoke like old men, reproaching in chirping toy voices the girls' indecency, their near-nakedness, accusing the girls of not wearing any bottoms. The girls' sweaters were big enough that they covered their rehearsal skirts, and while their tights were thick and ribbed, they were pale fleshy pink-beige. Combined with black cat-eyes and high boots, even low-heeled as they were, the girls looked to the boys like what they were not; maybe in 1966 they would have looked exactly like what the boys thought they were but it was not 1966, it was 1996. Young Ae beat the boys off with cool loud insults that the boys had not thought possible from the mouths of ballet dancers who looked like teenagers, but they were in fact half a decade older than that. The words and images that Young Ae used to attack the boys unfortunately insulted the female body and those of dogs, but also unfortunately, that is the only kind of insult that impresses most 15-year old boys. Throughout the harassment and its dispelling, Ji Eun stood in silence and yawned without opening her mouth.

Twenty years later, Young Ae's son yawned without opening his mouth, although he ended up being the fighting kind. Six years old, after being pushed around by a boy twice his size, Young Ae's son stabbed the boy near the eye with a sharpened pencil. Young Ae never knew whether her son's aim had been shitty or perfect, because while the boy twice his size was not blinded, he did bleed rather gruesomely. In the principal's office, the bully sat like a victim held in the embrace of his similarly hulking mother, his blood and tears spreading out into the bandage. Young Ae sat next to her son, touching the back of his hand with her own but not moving to hold it or otherwise perform comfort. Young Ae's son refused to explain, justify, or apologize, even though there were plenty of witnesses, both to his harassment and the method of victorious resistance. Young Ae took her son's cue fast and did not apologize to the mother of the bully or the bully himself, whose own silence seemed to be more shame than guilt. Whether it was self-defense or sadism, her son would not say, and never did. He had a few tears just dotting the corners of his eyes, not enough to wet his cheeks, and otherwise, seemed sleepy. Either way, the act was overwrought in the way of an unrealistic looking hothouse flower. She felt rather proud of her son then, and such pride did not feel all that perverse.

In the years that followed, that yawning silence became a part of Young Ae's son's general makeup. It turned his little cluster of cells into the physicality of a hard, little, wet statuette, a clay figure that looked as though it could never dry but would never lose its shape. In fact, this is how Young Ae saw her son: small, dense, slippery. But by the time he was 12 years old, he had gone from being like a statuette to statuesque. The summer before, he had begun forbidding anyone from seeing his body in its living skin, particularly his torso. He insisted on wearing long sleeves and pants year round. In the Bay Area, it was easy to get away with this. He could refuse to swim or go to the beach because the desire to go to the beach was never pressing, and because neither Young Ae nor her husband were enthusiastic swimmers and it didn't occur to them that it might be a life-saving skill their kid should learn, even though both could swim themselves.

But since they moved to Iowa City last summer, Young Ae's son took to hugging himself. Young Ae had been accepted to the Writer's Workshop, and while she began writing her poems in earnest, her doctorate dissertation lay in the deep dark recesses of her laptop's hard drive, curled, its chapters, some of them stopped mid-sentence even, unbegotten as the smooth stump-tipped limbs of a monstrous fetus, and outside it all, the heat of a true summer attacked her whole family with weird vengeance. But at least the cells of the bodies of Young Ae and her husband had memories of it. Their son and dog, however, were vaguely in shock. On the day the temperature hit 97 degrees, Marilyn ran out of the house into the yard in interest and excitement. This was rare because as an old dog now, Marilyn rarely ran with the manic zest and speed with which she used to play as a young thing. "The heat must have a different smell," Young Ae observed out loud. And she was right, because Marilyn's nostrils hummed wildly as she settled near the backdoor, her snout stretched stylishly into the humidity. But that took all of fifteen minutes before she sauntered into the shade and the concrete steps, and then back into the house, where she weirdly hovered under Young Ae's kitchen chair the entire day. Eventually, this place became her bomb shelter of summer. Young Ae's son, on the other hand, was finally forced to wear short sleeves and shorts. Neither Young Ae nor her husband forced him but the temperature was unbearable, even for that small obstinate human thing.

The hugging himself thing started when, as a lark, the family ventured for the first and only time to the city park pool. The entire time he was there, naked above baggy red swim shorts, he wrapped his arms tightly around his naked torso. When Young Ae suggested he take a dip in the shallow end, he refused, and when she suggested he unwrap himself, he actually emitted a moan, loudly in protest, as if he would die if his tiny, petal-pink nipples were exposed. From that day forward, he hugged himself even when he was clothed; it became his default pose. Paradoxically, there was in the kid's strange and repressive modesty a palpable drive to be a voluptuary. The way he pressed his torso with his forearms was exactly the way sex-comedy actresses in the 1950s held their melon-breasts out of a fear and desire that they overflow. As they did with most "Problems," Young Ae and her husband didn't confer officially about this, but individually, both felt there was something indecent about this drive of their kid's. But being who they were, they said nothing and let their son become weirdly voluptuous, statuesque.

In fact, they could say nothing because both of them acted like children themselves when their son came to them complaining of pain in his nipples. Young Ae had drawn his shirt up, looked at his little but healthy birdchest, and turned dumbly to her husband: "Do men also develop in their chests during puberty?" Equally dumbly, her husband had responded, "I don't know." Their son had stood there with a totally indecipherable look, his little grey t-shirt hitched up like a stuck bra. Young Ae looked with impassive aggression at her husband's gentle exasperation, and they scowled visibly at one another.

One October evening, Young Ae's son wore a light-weight turtleneck sweater made of gross-feeling, bumpy knit polyester. It had a cute stripey pattern but the particular shades of its white, blue and black stripes were horrendous. It had been Young Ae's shirt from the early '90s. It was ugly and Young Ae had stuffed it somewhere—back of the drawer, behind the washing machine—with the intention of turning it into a rag. Who knows how and where the kid dug it up, but he obviously loved it, and wore it as often as he could. As he was walking to the bathroom to brush his teeth, Young Ae called out to him to hand over the shirt to toss into the laundry hamper; it was soiled from too many days of continuous wearing. As he was taking his shirt off, his upper arms held as usual over his chest, Young Ae saw bruises, golden and violet, clearly old bruises coated over with fresh ones, blotched all across his arms so as he held himself, they became the shoulder-baring flounces of a Southern Belle.

Young Ae demanded—softly—where the bruises had come from. Her son responded with one tight word: "Nowhere." Young Ae was suddenly struck then that her son looked exactly like the best friend she hadn't thought of for years—Ji Eun was here again. His black hair, thick bangs poking his eyes and the edges hanging almost to his shoulders, made his skin look blue. Young Ae suddenly remembered that a blunt kind of bob was Ji Eun's favorite hairstyle. The kid who looked like Ji Eun stood with his neck pitched forward slightly but definitively in a pose that made his head exaggerated and vulnerable. His mouth was slightly open, but no breath moved in or out of him. The parted lips formed a thin line of soft black, as if words had just taken leave. Young Ae got a sense that her son was focusing his face so hard that the small body underneath the collarbones were being blurred away. But even through this self-willed blur she could see that there were more bruises over his ribs. He turned away, scuttled calmly with the steps of a geisha into the bathroom and turned the lock.

The last time she or her husband tried to protect their son from the outside world ended with a single mother being called a cunt. Granted, the single mother's daughter had been torturing Young Ae's son by teaching other third graders that he was a "faggot," but as much as Young Ae herself wanted to go over to the bitch's place and punch her and her daughter in the stomach, she didn't think that the woman deserved to pick up the phone and hear a crazed, angry man at the other end of the line screaming curses and threats. Earlier that day, Young Ae and her husband had sat in the office of the principal who told them with bared condescension that this is "how kids are," and while of course, the girl would be admonished, after all, it's not as if their son had been beaten up or something by this girl who was in fact, even shorter and slighter than him. As Young Ae and her husband opened their mouths to speak in fury, the principal coolly informed them that their son had actually made some drawings of the girl-bully that were not just anatomically correct but quite sophisticated in the torture it depicted. Young Ae and her husband closed their mouths, still fuming but confused.

The morning after seeing her kid's bruises, Young Ae put him on the school bus, precisely counted out a few hours, and although it was too warm a fall day for it, belted up her vintage Max Mara coat, long, caramel, cashmere, and pulled on strange boots that were 12 inches of narrow cones of dark grey wool felt on top and rubberized black leather feet with black heavy rubber soles. The boots had arrived just the previous evening via UPS from a shop in Los Angeles. Dressed thus, feeling armored or prepared as hazmat, Young Ae got ready to drive over to her son's elementary school. Marilyn expressed her usual sweet silent judgment on being left alone; she circled Young Ae with longing, looking bloodthirsty. Young Ae was suddenly hit by an unbearable love for her old dog. Marilyn was still as blond as ever, but her face had gone white and her once black nose now was almost pink. But she still had her childish interest in every small thing in the world, and still moved with her signature undulation: her back legs were disproportionately long, lifting the latter half of her body ever so slightly; when you watched her trot, from the back she looked jacked up, like a car with a flat tire getting ready by the side of the road, and she swung her butt purposefully, the back half of her body in a rhythm in lovely contrapuntal to the front half. She swung out thus behind Young Ae as far as the garage door, but once she realized Young Ae was getting into the car, she lost interest and plopped down on her stomach: Marilyn had a lifelong fear of cars. Young Ae would have liked to bundle her into the passenger seat for moral support but respected Marilyn's emotions.

Once on her way, Young Ae found a stale pack of Djarums in the glove compartment. She couldn't think of whose they were, since both she and her husband quit smoking years ago and besides, she smoked Marlboro Reds and he, American Spirits Blues. She took out a shitty-tasting cigarette, lit it and puffed, and tried not to think of the word "molest." That was hard. Surely those bruises could not be the result of some teacher or janitor rubbing his cock on her pure, penetrable son? She knew penises don't leave bruises, no matter how hard they get. But so what? So what if her son was not molested? It looked to her as if someone had been pressing into him with skin-covered bone or baseball bat or hard rope. And the rainbow bruises showed that it was something that had happened, or was happening, with some regularity. Luckily, Young Ae's imagination had a safety gasket. At that moment, it melted and sealed the wild feelings inside her. Her weird boots made her a terrible driver, unable to feel very well neither brake nor accelerator, so she focused on maneuvering the car, and still, twice almost got into an accident.

Finally she parked the car in the backlot of an office building that faced the front of the school from across the street. She got out and rested against the side of the car. It was a big old Chevy Impala from the 1970s, deep peach color with a thick slash of hot neon orange on the driver's side; a piece of her hip fit perfectly into the groove of the dent it covered. Young Ae rested as Hollywood actresses in the 1930s rested on slant boards with fat padded arm-rests that prevented mussing of costumes between scenes. She didn't know where to not look. In her long coat and strange boots, eyes hovering over an elementary school in broad daylight, she felt like a pedophile or flasher, as if she were bare naked underneath the coat, which was close to fact. Under the coat she was wearing her nightgown, which was really only a leopard-print, lace-edged half-slip and an old oversized t-shirt. When the noon bell rang she didn't see her son in the first pour of children. She didn't have to wait too long. It was a bit of a shock to see that her son didn't look so frail in the public context of school. Not that he looked any bigger or more substantial; he still looked as though he were a line drawing. He looked lonely, and he was alone. He was clutching a book that looked too big for his body. But he was holding it tightly against one hip like a handbag, and walking fearlessly towards nowhere. Instantly she thought: He probably has a perfect *pointe*.

Young Ae felt a need to run over, scoop her son up and throw him in the back of the Impala like a kidnapper; the feeling felt like a need to pee even though her bladder was bone-dry. Instead, she wound her free arm around herself loosely and trained eyes upon her son, and her head moved in abrupt micromovements like a surveillance camera. Her son walked around the playground sets that looked like the fixings of a cheerful S&M chamber, then to the edge of the yard and sat down behind a clump of thick trees. While Young Ae could clearly see where he was sitting, in a narrow patch of dirt between trees where the playground swerved up into a dirt hill, he was totally invisible to other kids on the playground.

A large person was walking slowly towards her son. Using her ballet training, Young Ae ran quietly and swiftly across the street to the edge of the yard and hid, probably completely ineffectively, behind a lamppost. She took out her phone and snapped a photo. Then she switched the camera mode to video and hit record. The person who was walking towards her son was skinny and almost as tall as she was, which was around 5'9", but this person was not an adult, but a boy, like her son. This boy was wearing a pullover in a surprisingly vibrant red that almost exactly matched Young Ae's son's. This boy had the wide shoulders of a man, but his long arms were gangly, a pup, and his head, large also like a puppy or a cartoon drawing or favorite teddy bear.

His skin was translucent and he already had adult hands growing from thin, child wrists. Black hair jutted out of the top of his head unevenly this way and that but it made him look adult—on the sides and back, it was shorn close, neat edges. His nose a cute button nose. Months after, she identified him as she and her son were perusing the annual class photo. In the photo, the boy's mouth was sneering and so were his eyes, squinting coquettishly and much too masculine for his age. His name: Ryan Wega. Young Ae assumed the name was a misprint for "Vega" until five years later when she saw his name and face again in the local newspaper: a high school student named Ryan Wega had been killed in a drug-related shooting.

As Ryan came towards him, Young Ae's son began standing up, the big book dropping to the ground. Young Ae's mouth opened, pre-scream, and she felt herself shake out from her dumb hiding spot, out of her dumb frozen flesh as she felt the mute instinct of an animal mother. But before he could stand completely, the other boy leaned down and scooped up Young Ae's son. The boy held her son, face to face. He held him, and she could see her son's body going perfectly limp against the bigger boy, arms and legs slack with the elegance of someone much older and needing something else, something more. Ryan planted his feet wide apart firmly and purposefully in the dirt and began to move them elegantly, and the pirouette began. He held her son so tight that he didn't have to hold Ryan back at all to stay aloft. The two spun, round and round, faster and faster. Ryan threw his head back, his neck bent in a frightening way, and Young Ae's son buried his face in Ryan's long collarbone. It was not quite sexual, but it was not childish either; it might have been romantic.

Young Ae's body finally produced a scream that was loud but so quick that it instantly became atmosphere. No one but the lamppost heard it. When Ryan put her son down, they were laughing with each other with a laughter that was secretive, but also clean. The boys looked into each other's eyes, and Young Ae's son put his hands on the other boy's shoulders as he was put gently back down on his own feet. Ryan picked up the heavy book from the ground and swinging it easy in his left hand, they walked out of their crawlspace together, almost hand-in-hand, up the hill away from the playground and Young Ae. They didn't seem afraid, ashamed, or furtive. Before they disappeared into the horizon, Young Ae could see Ryan say something to her son and her son responding with a giggle that she recognized, but it was not her own. But it was someone's giggle; it was Ji Eun's. Young Ae's mind couldn't pinpoint this memory but her body knew: the old t-shirt she used as a nightgown, the one she was wearing underneath her coat, was a raspberry colored Black Dog Tavern t-shirt she had bought back in 1994. The ballet academy had taken a trip to Boston, and there had been a weekend visit to Martha's Vineyard. Young Ae was eighteen years old, and so was Ji Eun. Each bought the same shirt: raspberry extra large. On the trip, they wore it as nightgowns together. Back in Seoul, also together, they wore it with jeans or short pleated mini-skirts with rows of buckles and black leather tabs at the hips. One year after Young Ae and her husband adopted Marilyn, they found online a DIY project for making a dog toy-slash-modular-slash-hammock. You'd put some thin slats of wood together in the shape of a table without a table top and stretch an old t-shirt or sweater around it so that the dog can lay on top, or in the interior of the shirt, suspended in the air, a womb and a hammock. The website recommended that you use an old shirt or sweater with a special scent association for the dog so it could be its extra special comfort place. Young Ae adored the idea of t-shirts she slept in or old sweaters she sat around in becoming Marilyn's return to a new womb, Young Ae's womb. However, neither Young Ae nor her husband were handy with tools or the Home Depot, so they improvised with an old chair that Young Ae had bought before she married. It was a small chair made of heavy wood, with thick legs and seat but a long, delicately slatted backrest with a wide curved top part that was painted with lambs and roses. It was obviously a child's chair but was painted the most queer shade of green that made you think of illness. But you couldn't strip the paint without stripping off the lambs and roses, so they practiced tolerance. Young Ae stretched her then favorite shirt-nightgown—the raspberry Black Dog Tavern shirt—over the legs of the chair and set it on its back on the floor. Not having built the thing to its specifications, Marilyn couldn't really suspend herself in a new womb but went bonkers over it nonetheless. Often, she would retreat into the t-shirt-womb and just rest there in a tight ball. Had the shirt been one of those navy-and-white French striped numbers, it would have looked as if there was a tapioca ball the size of a medium-sized dog lodged in the cheery straw of a bubble tea. They had taken it apart in the move and kind of forgot to put it back together. Young Ae had re-found the raspberry shirt among the dog stuff and was stunned by its softness and smell: it smelled of dog, herself, but also something else. Because then, she had not thought about Ji Eun for so long, she couldn't know that

Ji Eun thought about Young Ae every time she put on her own raspberry t-shirt. When Young Ae saw her son giggle in that way with Ryan, she couldn't remember Ji Eun's face or voice or laughter, or the intolerable vulnerability of her small, squared off scapulae, nor could she imagine Ji Eun's feelings. So she only walked back to the Impala and stood a little, apart, and stared hard at the hot neon orange. It's pretty, she thought. She said softly, but aloud, "It's pretty."

THE DINGO

The tiny, sugar-granule nipples of a spayed pup: they look like innocent (non-cancerous) moles on human surfaces, usually at the back of the neck, crevice of a collarbone or inside of the thigh, and just as insensitive as the spayed pup's nipples, the clinging remnants of puppyhood amidst an otherwise adult body, and all the more sweeter because they are so completely insensitive, purely decorative as the sugar dots on a broad field of buttercream atop a cake. Buttercream or eye cream? In these days of rose-infused dessert and honey-infused cosmetics, it's difficult to tell them apart, even with your tongue: one may as well frost the cake with Shiseido Benefiance Wrinkle Resist 24, as soft, pink and inviting as normative confection. But best not to dab buttercream on the suddenly thinning skin under one's eyes.

+

A dog is like a beautiful long bead: the expressive black swirls of the nostrils seem to lead uninterrupted, tubular, in toward the pink asshole that is so expressive when getting ready to void.

+

Pulling a resting dog towards you as you would a flower you want to enjoy but don't want to pluck.

+

I used to date a girl who seemed equally passionate about dogs and babies. This girl, Tasha, was very intelligent, much smarter than me, and intelligent in that self-aware, louche way I'm really attracted to. Because of her, I still associate intelligence with kinkiness; there wasn't anything she wouldn't try, provided we were both naked. She wasn't like some girls, who sucked your cock or let you fuck them up the ass as religious experience. Holiness is next door to guilt-tripping: begrudging tolerance before doing it, then using it as emotional or material leverage after. I sucked a cock once and it was actually kind of difficult, so I appreciate that, but it wasn't gross. I've never been fucked up the ass though, and I don't have a vagina, so I don't know, maybe it does deserve status as religious experience. Maybe if Tasha and I had stayed together longer she might have fucked me up the ass with a dildo or something; I certainly could have been talked into it by her. Anyway, Tasha sucked my cock and opened her ass to me with complete nonchalance. I liked that she didn't approach sex like it was some kind of exchange, but more like a shared physical activity, like hacky-sack or frisbee. Her entire vibe was, if she had to acknowledge that there might be anything demeaning in any sexual act, that acknowledgment would put a crack in her brilliant milky diamond skin. But this girl was obsessed with becoming pregnant.

"Not now, of course. But I don't kid myself; I know I want to have children. I *long* to care for another being, to lose myself completely in that feeling. To truly forget who you are in devotion to the protection of another... doesn't that feeling seem divine? Some women talk about not wanting to have children because they don't want to give up a career or their own selfishness, which, you know, I think every woman deserves because it's hard-earned in this world—selfishness, I mean. I admit I have a strong aspect of that feeling. But there are women—artists, writers, intellectuals—who have children so they can write about motherhood, or play mothers on stage. I think Sylvia Plath wanted to have children to write poems about being a mother. I have a strong aspect of that, also. But for me, I don't want a child so I could become some dumb mythic earth-mother bullshit figure. I don't want to have a child so I could bolster myself up into an even bigger protagonist of my life. I want to have a child so I can become an interesting supporting character in a life more interesting and qualitatively better than my own. You know?"

I shrugged and chomped at the pear I was eating for breakfast. I didn't shrug to be an asshole or anything. I shrugged because she said almost the exact same thing about dogs. Almost.

"I really wish I could keep a dog. But I can't kid myself, not right now. I just don't have enough energy or time or space for it. Oh but I *adore* dogs so much. Someday. There is something so essentially helpless about them, don't you think? Those eyes, the wet, tender squishy nose. I would love to lose myself in caring for a creature who is so utterly dependent on me. Can you imagine these jerks who tie up their dogs, train them to fight other dogs, neglect their dogs, even beat their dogs? Can you imagine a human who is low enough to beat a dog? You know I'm not a violent person *at all*, I so believe in peace, but if I ever see a person beat a dog, I promise I will do everything my body can do to destroy that person, on the spot."

I can still picture her, going on like this, in bed or at the kitchen table, one leg always drawn up, arm resting on her knee, fingers dangling either a menthol cigarette or a candy bar, one of those miniature ones that you hand out to kids on Halloween. She told me her feelings about dogs after we had been dating a few months, and I had figured I might as well get serious as not. So I said: "Well, I like dogs a lot. I've always wanted one but my mother would never let me or my brothers get one. I know you can't get one because you live in the dorm, but we could get one together and keep it at my place since I live off campus?" I looked out the window. I was sitting on my bed, which was just a cheap mattress on a matching box spring on the floor. It was almost summer, and the backyard was yellow with dead grass but I thought it looked kind of nice, like corn. This backyard was just a square patch of usually dead grass with a metal trash container in one corner. It wasn't fenced off and led directly into a soft hill of a driveway that wasn't too safe for dogs off-leash. But I felt like I could make it work.

"Do we want to be that serious?"

I shrugged. "Aren't we already?"

"What kind of dog do you want?"

"I don't know. Doesn't matter to me. We could look up what rescue shelters are round here and drive up one night or weekend and look around, see what cuties we can find."

"But I'm really set on a French Bulldog. I'm pretty sure you couldn't find one at a rescue shelter. They're a very expensive and exclusive breed."

"Oh. Why a French Bulldog?"

"They look so poetic. Their smashed face makes them like a monster, but they are built so petite and holdable."

"Well, OK. But we could still go look, just in case? You never know, you know."

We never did make it over to the rescue shelter but I did find out the real reason Tasha wanted a French Bulldog: some designer, either Yves Saint Laurent or Karl Lagerfeld, I can't remember which, had one. Like a lot of college students, Tasha was nimble with both the fashionable and philosophical. She made her love of French Bulldogs seem deeply personal. But the French Bulldog is not a person; it's not even an individual, as in an individual dog; it's just a type, a breed, a category, an abstraction of a dog. She acted as if she loved the way the French Bulldog looked, which would have been aestheticism in a deeply personal way. In fact, she just loved the idea of the French Bulldog. She wanted that breed of dog to be an avatar. Which is also fine, but I think it would have been better if she thought she looked like a

French Bulldog, and wanted a dog that reflected her. That kind of narcissism to me is dumb but honest. Instead, I think she wanted a vibe of sophistication and fashionability in just owning a French Bulldog, rather than actually being around it all the time. I think those are different things.

We were both in our early twenties then. She was very pretty. When I met her we were both freshmen in college, in neighboring dorms, typical friends-of-friends thing. She looked like a young girl in old movies, with bubbly eyes and long dark hair. I can't remember what I looked like. We were both trying to act all knowing but failing. When we met again our junior year at a party, she had her hair cut off to shoulder length and dyed jet-black. Her skin looked paler with that black hair. I think she was wearing lipstick the color of her skin because it looked like she had no mouth. And around her eyes were thick black lines that swerved up almost to her temples. She had gotten much thinner, and she was fairly thin before. With the black hair, no mouth, black holes for eyes, body that seemed so thin it reminded me of TV static, she looked a little sick. The way she looked made me excited. She was in a totally different movie now than two years earlier, and I wanted to be in that movie with her. We decided to go for coffee the day after that party, and we dated for almost a whole year.

+

As far as the rescue shelter veterinarian Dr. del Olano could see, the dog was a pup, approximately seven months old, and possibly a mix of Australian Cattle Dog, Rat

Terrier, Beagle, and Golden Retriever. It seemed the terrier or beagle's genes had won out over the others in the size department because she was, at six months, rather on the small side. She had weirdly long and elegant legs, which to Young Ae and her husband looked like the legs of a deer. Also, they thought all puppies had huge feet, but hers were surprisingly dainty and narrow, joined seamlessly and elegantly parallel to the width of her ankles like hoofs. Neither Young Ae nor her husband knew what an Australian Cattle Dog or Rat Terrier looked like, but they knew about Beagles and Golden Retrievers, and those, they could see in her, especially the long, pointy Snoopy snout and blond fur. She had the ravishing blond fur of a Golden Retriever. The outer side of her floppy ears went almost in ringlets, as did the fur along her belly, her backside, even her ankles. Only her legs and feet were not totally blond: all marled they were, paint-white, and splattering of red-gold and blue-black.

Young Ae and her husband were sitting in a large room where prospective owners could make first contact with prospective companion species. Although the room was painted in bright, cheerful colors, Young Ae's husband called it a "holding cell" and Young Ae had to admit, he was right. The room was hung with the heavy silence of awkwardness and disappointment, and occasional yelps of the dogs pierced the air, sounding more like anxiety and fear than excitement—the genuine kind that precedes total slumber, peace, and relaxation. The room was moated by a concrete-floored walkway that was itself walled off by black wire caging holding the dogs in the individual holes of their desperation. The whole setup struck Young Ae as quite Foucauldian, except it was difficult to tell who was activating the panopticon, the jailed dogs or the jailor humans but that in itself was perhaps Foucauldian. The blond deer-pup had been crated in that wall next to an old German Shepherd who clearly looked as though she were done with it all. Young Ae's husband had been interested in the German Shepherd for a moment.

"I wonder if she's a retired dog actor. German Shepherds are in movies all the time. Maybe this one spent her entire life playing dogs of Nazis and pigs and white supremacists, and she's just sick of all of it," he said to Young Ae.

"Maybe," she replied, not really listening because already all her attention was focused on the blond pup next door, who displayed the same world-weary affect.

"What would you name her?" Young Ae asked her husband. It struck her suddenly that in planning for this day, they had never together fantasized about a cute name. The dog was now sitting between them, tail end at Young Ae's husband. The dog's face was turned away from Young Ae and it looked blankly out into the claustrophobic nowhere. Young Ae reached over, stroked the dog's delicate front paw and held it lightly. The dog shook with its whole body and pulled away from her.

"I don't know. I don't think I'm good with names."

"Is it silly to name her something that has to do with being blond? Because she's so blond. Like Marilyn? Or maybe something less obvious, like Catherine, pronounced 'Katrin' for Catherine Deneuve. Oh that is so pretentious and stupid?"

"Well, it's not stupid. They already named her 'Buttercup,' which is something about being blond, or yellow, I guess, and stupid."

"I kind of like Marilyn."

"Sounds like the name of an old woman from the Bronx."

"I don't know. I like the sound of it, somehow."

"It's fine by me." The words were indifferent, but his tone was somewhat warm and sympathetic. He added, "She's beautiful. I guess we're taking her."

The dog was frightened and curious. Her ears were so flattened against her head in a way that made her look wet, and she had slinked tightly into a corner. But she allowed both humans to touch her chin, chest, and after a few minutes of cooing baby-voiced jibber jabber, head, albeit at a safe distance: both Young Ae and her husband had to stretch to pet her. Young Ae's husband found a little valley of space on her skull above her eyes and with his left ring finger, he stroked with a stunning kind of gentleness that made the dog's eyes nearly close. Even though the dog was clearly wary of them and regarded them with dilated pupils filled with a look that contained fear and suspicion that still managed to be judgmental, Young Ae felt a pang of petty jealousy as she watched her husband stroke the dog's head; it seemed to her that the dog was already sort of oriented towards her husband.

The actual process of adoption seemed interminable, although five hours of one's day seems speedy compared to the process of adopting a human baby. At least that's what Young Ae and her husband told each other cuddling over their dog at home that night. Young Ae and her husband had imagined that they would fill out some papers— name, address, phone number, maybe occupation?—and that would be that. Instead, they were escorted, or rather, herded, with a gang of other prospective pet owners, into a whole other section of the building that resembled an office where very annoying but mandatory-to-life trans-actions took place: a wall of narrow service windows, and above it, a digital number sign. All the uncomfort-able fiberglass chairs in the waiting area were taken up, so Young Ae and her husband sat on the floor and stared at their number which they felt would never come up. Once it did, they went up to file their papers, and were told to wait again while the veterinarian prepared medical release papers and references listed in the adoption application were contacted and questioned.

Young Ae and her husband had been surprised by the "References" section in the application but had assumed it was a formality. Young Ae's husband put down the name of a college buddy. Young Ae had put down the name of another graduate student in her class because it was the easiest per-son she could think of. But she only knew the woman from a couple seminars, and she couldn't bear the idea of her receiving a call from the dog shelter on Young Ae's behalf.

"Actually, can I give you a different reference? I would rather you call someone I've known longer," she said to the clerk at the window.

Young Ae scratched out the graduate student's name and scribbled in that of a dancer from her old days in the *corps*. They weren't best friends or anything, but he was a sweet gay guy and they had gone out for drinks. He'd invited her over to his and his partner's home multiple times. She scanned through her address book frantically and was relieved to find his number was still there.

Then it was back to their space on the floor.

"You never had a dog, so you wouldn't know this, but I still remember certain looks that my mother's dog used to get," Young Ae said to her husband.

"That old Jindo dog?"

"Yes, Mary. Well, no. I don't know. My mother loved dogs and she had like four consecutively. They were all the same kind of Jindo dogs—all white, all pointy ears, black eyes, pink nose, tall, muscular, big fat tails—and I swear, I could never tell when one actually died because you know, when their time comes they die kind of slowly, and my mother would cry a little bit every day during those days so when the dog finally died, there was no big release of tears or anything. And dogs are so stoic you can't even tell sometimes they are sick. But my mother would get a replacement dog so fast, it seemed one day the dog was dead and then the next, there'd be another one that looks exactly like the first. And on top of that my mother called every one of her dogs 'Mary.' It's like she just had one dog in her head or heart that took different physical forms. The last Mary she had, before my mother herself died, was stolen. Someone actually climbed over the wall—you know those old Korean houses, the walls aren't that high, but still—and took her in the night. My mother was so devastated. I've never seen her cry like that. I think she was so angry that she couldn't go out and protect poor Mary, but she was so sick by that time. Have you ever seen a dog look at you to let you know they understand you're angry? Even when you're not angry at them but at someone else? If you see that look on their face, you want to never feel the emotion of anger ever again."

Four hours later, finally in the car and on their way home, Marilyn (Buttercup) vomited into Young Ae's husband's lap. Instantly, Young Ae thought of tiny black stitches on the pup's white, lightly spotted belly, and how that spot, where she had been recently spayed, must be so raw or irritating. Young Ae reached over to touch Marilyn's head and accidentally brushed the vomit. The puke was weirdly cool to the touch, the chunks perfect as pearls clinging to the putty-colored liquid. Even though they were driving over the Bay Bridge when Marilyn puked, Young Ae pulled over onto the shoulder as if they had been in a car accident, and got out of the car. Young Ae's husband didn't move, as though he were pinned to the spot by car wreckage, although it was only a 15-pound puppy. Marilyn's puke was seeping through his clothes but he remained completely indifferent to the yucky feeling. He sat still and watched Young Ae. She was moving very slowly around the front of the car to come to his side and to him looked as though she wanted to be alone. For some reason she stopped for a second, and in that moment, she looked like a scene in a Western he'd seen once, long ago: the vulnerable but tough prairie woman, bonnet cocked back to the small of her neck like a tough guy's hoodie. Young Ae's resemblance was intensified because she was wearing a strange outfit she had just bought: a knee-length coat in thick wool, wide trousers detailed to look like jeans at the waist and hip pockets, and a hooded sweater made out of boiled wool and cashmere. All three pieces were designed by a major French house, and all three were in a deep shade of magenta that made her look like a very narrow glass of wine or a long blood drop. The sweater had a queer zippered neck that when open, made her look like a soccer mom, but when zipped up created a tight turtleneck that turned the hood into a balaclava. When she put the hood over her head, though, as she did now, she looked like a pioneer woman of Oregon, California, or Outer Space.

Young Ae obligingly and gracefully opened the door and moved around to let her husband out. She reached over and undid the seatbelt. They transferred Marilyn between them in silence and he got out of the car. With the backside of his hands, he scraped off the puke, which seemed to float a bit before hitting the ground. Some pearls and chunks clung because he was not too meticulous in his big sloppy chopping motions. So there was a large wet butterfly stain. But that didn't make him look like he peed his pants; rather, it looked as though someone who had just peed squatted over him and just sat down. Young Ae's husband shrugged a little and wiped his hands on his butt.

Young Ae said without an admonishing tone: "Why did you do that? Now you've spread your mess."

Again, he shrugged, even littler this time. "It's fine, I don't care about my clothes. I just didn't want the dog to sit in her own puke." It was a chilly evening but Young Ae's husband wore only a black tennis shirt and black Carhartt pants. When he bent over you could see a bit of his green boxers, patterned with little Dr. Seuss fish.

"But suppose she vomits again. Here." Shifting Marilyn from one arm to the other, Young Ae slipped off her coat and handed it to him. "Put this on your lap."

"It's fine. You don't need to ruin your new coat."

"It's fine. Actually, it would give it a nice patina, a patina of our new life as dog parents. Besides…." Her tone, which was beginning to get simultaneously nagging and provocative, went creamy, back into her body. "It feels kind of nice, like she's bonding with me."

"OK." Young Ae waited until her husband got back in the car, deposited Marilyn back into his arms, and closed the passenger side door. Again, Young Ae felt jealous and as small as the feeling was, it worried her. She ached for Marilyn, who was a small blond pile of emptiness that two people were starting to shoot through with their strange human feelings. If they were lucky, Marilyn would be a medium-sized dog. If they were unlucky, Marilyn would become the little steering switch in the belly of a huge and vulnerable battleship.

Several weeks earlier, Young Ae's husband mentioned to his mother during a rare telephone call that he and Young Ae were planning to adopt a puppy. Her initial silence was long and disapproving, and actually caught him by surprise. He knew that his mother didn't like dogs, and he knew she didn't believe in adoptions. But he couldn't believe she was actually going to make something out of it.

"You must think carefully about this," she finally said.

"It's just a dog. It's not as if we are adopting a child. Or even having a child, biologically."

"If you two don't want children, I guess that's your choice. The incorrect one, but your choice. But why then do you need another thing to spend your love on? You must focus on Young Ae. She is the most important thing in your life right now, especially because you don't have a real job."

"I don't know why you think about love as a can of stuff to be used up. I have more than enough for my wife *and* a dog." As soon as he spoke the words they felt dumb, yet true.

"Because love makes you tired. Don't you know that yet?"

"No. It doesn't make me tired. It's obvious it's made you tired."

"You shouldn't talk to me like this. Listen to your mother, and think carefully about this decision. It is just an animal. It has no consequence. You are going to spend too much time with this animal that will bring you nothing at the end."

Young Ae's husband wondered what he, as a human thing to his mother, was expected to bring to her. He couldn't guess at all.

"I'm pretty sure that I've brought you nothing in the end, and I'm a human and your biological child," he continued. "I'm not sure that Young Ae will bring me anything real at the end, either. And Mom, I'm actually OK with that."

Now, he couldn't remember whether he had hung up with those words or if it was his mother who had hung up on him. As they set off again, in peace and puke, Young Ae said to her husband, her voice thrilled: "I hope we don't just totally fuck it up."

The dog vomited again, but this time, Young Ae's husband insisted they just drive on home; Marilyn (Buttercup) was shaking almost as if epileptic. They were all three tired from the day but OK with that. The woman processing the adoption application had told Young Ae and her husband that they would have to wait at least a few hours, so it's not like they were caught off guard. Young Ae and her husband had driven to a deli nearby to get packaged salads for lunch, then went on to the pet store next to the shelter to prepare for their future. The shop was tiny but surprisingly well-stocked, albeit with relatively cheap goods. They bought an abstract purple squeaking toy with the rich, glossy synthetic coat of Orlon; an electric blue Nylabone with little nubby thorns that looked vaguely menacing; a small bag of puppy food (they chose the brand that featured the most excitable looking puppy on the bag); a canister of Milk Bones; a collapsible crate made of oxidized wire; and two metal feeding bowls that had a strange, otherworldly beauty. All this stuff sat calmly in the trunk of the car.

Marilyn (Buttercup) had no personal history before she was carried into the car of Young Ae and her husband. Even the dumb name Buttercup had been given to her by the shelter employees having sweet harmless thoughtless fun logging her into the system: the other dogs in her rescue group were named Tulip, Daisy, Rose, and Hyacinth. She had been born in and transported from Tennessee but no one could tell Young Ae and her husband who, if anyone, had owned her; if she had sisters and brothers; if she had been abused and neglected, or loved but simply surplus.

ACKNOWLEDGMENTS

I would like to express my gratitude to my sister Meenha Lee and my mother Jeung Hee Kang; at Nightboat Books, Stephen Motika, Andrea Abi-Karam, Caelan Nardone, and Lindsey Boldt; for the look of the book: Brian Hochberger and Catherine Homans; my colleagues and students at RISD; my loyal and true friends Tracy Steepy, Chi-ming Yang, Patricia No, and Antonia Pinter; our lovely Nella. And I give all my love to my steady love, Roddy Schrock.

JOON OLUCHI LEE lives and writes in femininity and feminism. The author of two works of fiction, *94* (2015) and *Lace Sick Bag* (2013), as well as various essays on queer theory, feminism, and fiction writing, Joon is Associate Professor of Gender Studies and Creative Writing at Rhode Island School of Design. He lives in Brooklyn with his partner Roderick Schrock and their rescue dog Nella.

NIGHTBOAT BOOKS

Nightboat Books, a nonprofit organization, seeks to develop audiences for writers whose work resists convention and transcends boundaries. We publish books rich with poignancy, intelligence, and risk. Please visit nightboat.org to learn about our titles and how you can support our future publications.

The following individuals have supported the publication of this book. We thank them for their generosity and commitment to the mission of Nightboat Books:

Kazim Ali
Anonymous
Jean C. Ballantyne
Photios Giovanis
Amanda Greenberger
Elizabeth Motika
Benjamin Taylor
Peter Waldor
Jerrie Whitfield & Richard Motika

In addition, this book has been made possible, in part, by grants from the New York City Department of Cultural Affairs in partnership with the City Council and the New York State Council on the Arts Literature Program.